THE
DREAMLAND TREE

THE
DREAMLAND TREE

Michael Standen

HEINEMANN : LONDON

William Heinemann Ltd
15 Queen Street, Mayfair, London W1X 8BE
LONDON MELBOURNE TORONTO
JOHANNESBURG AUCKLAND

First published 1972
© Michael Standen 1972

Printed in Great Britain by
Northumberland Press Ltd., Gateshead

I. M. Isobel Ogier 1918

Sleep, baby, sleep,
Thy father guards the sheep,
Thy mother rocks the dreamland tree.

NURSERY RHYME

BOOK ONE

ONE

A child's cough. *Ka-ka*. Impatient, undisguised and sounding dire. T.B. Whole grey streets clicked under William's eyelids. Where grandma lived. It would only be one of the smaller Ansteys though, built like tanks. That was one of his mother's comments to their mother—so he was thinking her thoughts.

But he had almost forgotten to check through his five senses. His own idea once a day to make a quick check. Sight. That was out because he refused to open. They would see only the blue of the sky and he liked the red of his eyelids better, or deep pinkiness. His sky. For sound there had been the little Anstey's cough and of course the sea—a few collapsing waves. Something about touch wasn't satisfactory. All of you was in touch all the time, if only with the air. It took ages to remember smell and when he had he couldn't summon strength to sniff. The sea again probably—tang, wasn't it? Jolly good it was warm. It was when you came to think about it, very. The grown-ups had announced it at breakfast. Now he let the sun's waves collapse over him. Science next year—that was this year!—at the High School. That explained everything. Something hopped in him, his heart. The deep pinkiness rippled a bit with the waves of the sun. Light waves he knew about already. The man, his father, had told him. He knew quite a lot.

Janet sat on a rock, a bereft queen. The little kids splashed about, making a lacy fuss at the edge. The horizon struck her as harder than in pictures. The blue hem of Britain. Queenly, she sat. A few years ago she had been their age. Now she was

3

much older. She wondered about having babies with a fore-taste of interest.

Hubert wanted to say something about his feet. He said, 'Look!' but they were fighting over the boat. His feet had a smaller look and when he looked he saw a shell on the bottom, a big one like an ashtray. He could pick it up and give it to daddy for his cigarettes, or put it away. He tipped it with one of his smaller feet. Things lived in them. But his toe had got there first; and the slug had gone away. They had shells like this in the shops and he had found it all by himself.

Then great splashing stars of water and he didn't have it.

'Look, look!' Tricia was jumping up and down, waving his shell.

'It's mine!' The water was heavy. Tricia danced on it with her long legs. 'I found it.'

'So did I,' she said. 'In your hand, ninny.'

'I *found* it,' he said. All the others were coming. She must tell them he had found it. But she jumped in the sea-stars.

'Look what I've got!'

His own big brother took it. 'Air-holes,' he said. 'It's all right for a shell.'

Trying to keep up, he couldn't. He wanted to tell John how his toe had plopped it for an ashtray. But all the others were there. It passed round and back into her hand. 'It's an ormolu.'

Tricia pointed to the inside which shimmered with colours: 'That's valuable pearl.'

'Mother of pearl,' said John.

'That's what I said.'

Hubert knew the shell, though he wasn't close; he knew it because it was his. Then the others ran off to daddy's cricket but Tricia stayed a bit, tall and jumping. Perhaps now she was going to give back the shell. In some funny way he knew she wouldn't, even whilst believing his parents' 'You've only to ask nicely.' He knew she had stayed behind because to the others it was only a shell to look at—they didn't know. But

4

he did and she did. Still, he wanted the shell.

'Do you want to see my ormolu?'

'No,' he said, banging flat hands on the water. 'It's not yours.'

'Is! I want you to look at it and then I want it back. If you don't, I'll duck you.' He had it, its airholes and mothery pearl. 'Duck you,' said Tricia. 'Do you know what that means?'

She was frightening. Hubert shook his head.

'Push your head under. Under here.' She flung some sea.

She was big and careless and would do it.

Hubert was nearly five years old and held the shell. But Mark was three, *he* was the baby. And the baby now as well —two smaller than him. The shell was his. At home he thought of things she could have instead.

'You've had your pennorth.'

The sun shone right down to his feet. Far away the big children were somewhere on the beach: they could do anything they wanted, if they wanted. And daddies. Up to his tummy in sea, Hubert knew as something new like going to London that no one was going to help him. He surrendered it into one of her dripping hands; it was still his. Tricia looked at it, but only as if she had to. With a long sweep of her big girl's arm she threw it out to sea.

'How's William Arthur?' It was Uncle George. Here! Uncle George pressed down on his head, scuffling hair.

'I'm all right, thank you.' His hands half raised themselves, half fell back. Of course there was no tie to straighten, no flannel shirt. He felt small and naked and before his mother had called he had been so large on the sand that he had been everything: the sky his pink eyelids, his hands horizons.

'Don't whisper down your chest,' said Uncle George, 'as if saying grace. Isn't that right, Meg? Straight out—I'm fine, or I'm bloody awful, as the case may be.'

'Leave him alone,' said his mother. 'And that's what my mother would call "language".'

Uncle George laughed and slapped him on the head. Bill hung it down, filled with Uncle George's tallness in a blazer, with his mother's look when telling Uncle George off, which had made it not a telling-off.

'I flew,' Uncle George announced. 'How about that? Whisked in by the Raf.'

'Which explains being so raffish, I suppose.'

'The things you suppose, Meg.'

Uncle George was saying about the island from the air. Bill lifted his vision; he could no longer ignore the fact that Uncle George had *flown*, coming in from the sky where the sun was. Sound. No remembered engines.

'From five thousand feet it's not big enough to blow your nose on, not even yours, miss.' Tricia was there, caught by the nose. But Tricia never minded Uncle George. 'We made two overshoots as it was. Give us that kids' spade, Meg.'

'Boys will be boys,' said his mother. He hated these phrases she never used at home.

'That's about the size of it.' Uncle George hacked a small triangle in the sand. 'From five thousand,' he said.

'It's like a map,' said Tricia.

'Glad you think so. See, we came in over Sark. The worst approach, apparently. The pilot said something about hot air.'

'You'd been chewing his hind leg off all the way over.'

'Watch it, Meg.'

'Did you drive the plane?'

'What's that? Not likely. I had a chauffeur.' The little Ansteys came over, deserting cricket. 'Ever tried putting a twin-engined Avro Anson down on a postage stamp?' Uncle George's hand, twin-engined, zoomed in from Sark and over-shot.

Tricia shook her head. He looked towards the sea and wished despite himself that the Avro Anson was out there sinking.

'Uncle George is speaking to you, Billy.' His mother. Her gentleness hit him. Blind, deaf, senseless—all stopped up.

Uncle Anstey, his real uncle, had come from cricket. The

6

horsepowered hand climbed away and they shook hands at their altitude. Uncle Anstey's specs flashed so that he was not to be seen behind them. At his gymshoes one little Anstey sputtered briefly as a plane.

'Try to be your age, Bill, if only to please me.' It was an appeal, mattering to her then whether he acted his age. The words didn't matter, what mattered was her dependence on him. He looked up in hope to where she sat beyond the dumpy shadow of the men and though her summer dress showed too much of her arms and chest he smiled a sort of sickly, reassuring smile. 'Have you been in yet? You used to rush in as soon as you saw the sea.'

'I'll go later.'

'Go now—I'll watch you.'

But he knew she would not, not from there. There was a fine wind of betrayal in the hot air. He stayed put and studied his uncles.

Farewell my realm, you will suffer long but with goodly patience. A thousand hearts beat true for me in the forest. I dedicate my Royalty to Sir Rommel Goodyear. I shall not look back.

Sir Rommel stood behind her, his armour stained with combat and his eyes with the pain of her going. They too were fixed on that hard dropping line dividing off the future, the exile of the future.

'Janet.'

She turned on her rock. William Goodyear with one of the awful Goodyear towels round his shoulders.

'What did you want to come barging in for?'

'They want us. That's what they sent me for.'

'You can tell them ...' She sighed. 'Don't bother.'

'It's not barging in,' he said doubtfully. 'It's barging in if it's a room—or a canal, I suppose.'

Janet realised that the sort of person she *could not stand* was boys of her own age. Curious that Sir Rommel had William's surname, but purely accidental. He had also been standing exactly on the spot occupied by Sir Rommel. Apart from his name, impossible for the part! Sir Rommel's tortured, loyal eyes were vanishing out to sea along the trails of their gaze.

'Haven't you got two names?'

'Arthur,' said William.

'Good job you're not Anstey. "Buzz, buzz, buzz, I'm a busy little bee." '

'We've all got rotten names.'

'Yes! Janet for example.'

'My great uncle was mayor of some place.'

'No, Arthur's all right. King Arthur, he was legendary. What do you think of when I say "Janet"?' If luck held he might be tolerable after all. Cousin Arthur ... put like that ... and the holiday which promised two aeons at least. She would test him. 'Think,' she commanded. 'Janet.'

'I don't know.'

'You can try, Arthur. You are a cousin. When you hear the word, what do you think of?'

'You, I suppose.'

Janet got up. 'Let's see what they want.' Carefully she resisted jumping from rock to rock and kicking through pools. She moved instead regally, despite difficulties. And he kept up awkwardly, in attendance. 'You' she decided as the pinkish rocks fined down to sand was not such a bad answer. Nothing —not specs, dumplings, nits—would have been bad enough for the name. Its true awfulness frequently astonished her. In fact 'you' was a bit complimentary as an answer. And there was what her father had said once about roses smelling as sweet. Reaching the welcome of sand she said in reckless reward: 'You can call me Eleanour. Is that all right? I'll call you Arthur. The others needn't know.'

She had immediate doubts. There he stood stirring the last rock-pool with a toe. Boys were capable of lunacies and for all that Eleanour was second best to the best, most private Aelfrida, she did not want it thrown around like the beach ball. Accordingly she kept a solemn eye on him as he stirred.

8

Not like her brother John—out all at once with reactions—his consideration of the proposal endowed him with some interest. Neither was Sir Rommel hasty of speech. The interest was different of course; they were not to be compared. Still, however perfect Sir Rommel's replies when they came, William's—Cousin Arthur's—promised something else to wait for: she couldn't know what he was going to say.

He said: 'The others will hear it when I call you.'

'Unless we keep it for when we're by ourselves like now.'

'You only need someone's name when you call them. So that means there'd be more than one. I mean I don't ever call Tricia by her name. I just say "you" like everyone else.'

'Well, I don't happen to agree.' Janet picked up a stone in her toes and plopped it in the pool. 'A rose smells as sweet but that doesn't mean you don't use names, Arthur. See, I've just used yours.' She glimpsed the final, clinching test lying ahead and picked it up. 'Call me mine and we'll go and join the others.'

'You can't just *say* it,' he said.

'Go on.'

'What?'

'The name, silly.'

'Eleanour?'

'Yes.'

'I've said it,' said William, being clever.

'No, you haven't. I can't wait all day.' Her foot transported another stone from its place in the warm sand. He watched it. 'Say it to me and look at me—that's all.'

He looked at her and she nodded. Standing on one foot made dignity difficult. The moment he said the name the other would drop its stone. Their eyes held on; her toes held on. Their eyes were like horizons. Toes were getting cramp. 'One ... two ... three,' she suggested.

'Eleanour,' he said. They both laughed. The stone swam down.

'See what they want,' she said.

9

To do something with the embarrassment they ran along the beach at immense speed.

'We need teams.' Uncle George threw the ball to spectacular heights, catching it. 'Bowlers and batters and whippets in the out-field. No excuses will be accepted. Ah, here's William A. and Janet, isn't it? Hullo, Janet. How's your leg break?'

With an unexplained pang Bill saw his mother attempting to settle bails on the stumps.

'Must I?' Janet shuffled on the sand.

'We've been organised,' said her mother, laughing.

'We're picking teams.' Tricia was everywhere. 'Uncle George is captain—and your daddy is captain as well.'

'Father will be thrilled,' said Janet with wasted sarcasm.

'And I'm on Uncle George's side. Uncle George said so.'

'Ansteys versus Goodyears.' John made a boy's-story drive to the covers and landed on his face.

Tricia objected. 'There's more of you and it's not fair and anyhow Uncle George isn't a Goodyear.'

Bill's objection was secret, almost to himself. He too swiped for the boundary but his hands moved hardly an inch. No one would guess how he had clouted Uncle George into the water. Now he was wild to start. Janet was hanging on her father's arm at a distance.

At last they were in a row and the rocketing ball in the blazer pocket. Both mothers exchanged grimaces at one end of the line whilst the other—Hubert and little Mark—disintegrated every two seconds. The baby sat like an umpire, eating sand.

'Toss?' Uncle George fished out a bright half-crown.

'If you think it's necessary.' Uncle Anstey hitched flashing specs.

'Heads!' Uncle George retrieved his coin. 'Our Lord and Sovereign right enough. My pick.'

Tricia ran out to hold his hand.

'Steady on.'

'All right. All yours, Jack.'

'Meg then.'

'Ooh er.' Uncle George pretended to be frightened. 'We don't stand an ice-cream's chance in Hades now.'

Bill watched his mother go to Uncle Anstey, sticking out her tongue as she passed Uncle George.

'Sucks!' screamed Uncle George. 'Our go now.'

Tricia was whispering advice. He bent his slicked and shiny hair for it. More than ever William wanted to be on his mother's side, to get Uncle George out first ball. The gleaming head shook. 'Liz.'

'Janet,' said Jack.

'John,' said George.

'Bill,' said Jack. William joined Uncle Anstey's team but his sister objected again: it wouldn't be fair—if Uncle Jack had Janet they ought to have William. 'It's ages,' she explained. 'There's Janet and William, they're the big ones and we ought to have one on our side.'

So he was beside the blazer when the coin flashed again for first in and George VI granted second victory. Everyone fielded, the little ones digging themselves miniature Anderson shelters in the out-field. Uncle George directed operations until Bill's mother pointed out that Uncle Anstey should be doing it.

He said: 'The sea's the boundary then.' It was. Soon, William thought, in a few hours, the pitch would be under the shiftless, shifty sea.

'Six if you knock it to France!' That face was red, unfaceable; that blazer so neat and large. 'Liz—opening bat.'

'First I knew Mummy played cricket.'

William was grateful for the conspiracy of Janet's passing remark. It made him feel less small and naked, almost grown-up, in charge at least of what was happening inside. A breath noise signified all this.

Aunty Liz missed her husband's slow lob. Uncle George showed her how to hold the bat, holding her and the bat. 'Elbow up.'

She hit the next one and while Hubert chased it amongst his feet ran on Tricia's orders.

The third bounced, scuttled up the bat and hopped off her elbow—to be next seen held aloft by a prostrate Uncle George. He got up, dusting a grain or two of sand from his blazer. 'Sorry, Liz. Couldn't resist it. Bowled Anstey, caught Straker. Your turn, young 'un.'

Bill squared up to Uncle Anstey. No pleasure in driving him out to sea. He looked to see who was looking. His mother was but Janet was trailing the sea's edge.

'Two legs,' said Uncle George, one of his mysteries. 'All set?'

Uncle Anstey brushed back black-grey hair, bowled and clean-bowled him. 'Have another go. Your eye wasn't in.'

Uncle George said: 'Ask no quarter, give no quarter, eh, Bill?'

'It's all right.' Truly he did not mind; Janet's opinion of the game was advertised in tideline footprints.

'That's cricket,' said Uncle George in the tones of a great truth, taking the bat. At the other end the bowler was walking away. William walked away. It looked as if Uncle George would be left high and dry. But the ball came bouncing wide from someone else. 'Aim at me, Meg.' Uncle George clipped it back.

He willed his mother to get him out. Her tongue, he guessed, was between her teeth, the trademark of her concentration. Down it came more on course and got the chop, a real crack.

'Swim for it somebody!' The batsman stopped running and claimed a six. Janet was alerted with shouts. She had walked away from the game but Uncle George had sent it after her. He had made the tide flow back to him. He spat on his hands, joked with the little ones. For the next few minutes bat and blazer dominated. The score soared. Every bowler was tried, right down to little Hubert. Often the ball bobbed in with the breakers. If he was on the other side! He imagined sly

12

spinners, Australian twisters hunting out the target.

Uncle Anstey remained quietly unenthusiastic but tried setting a field. In his indestructibility Uncle George towered. He was the life and soul, winning over those like Tricia who needed no winning, those like John and Aunt Liz. His own mother? William was sure only of Janet, of himself and half-sure—because he was a grown-up—of Uncle Anstey. Together they resisted the mastery of Uncle George.

Now she was bowling again; it was wrong, a woman bowling overarm. She was doing better, almost well sometimes, and the ball took fewer flights towards France. In other circumstances, he might have prided in her. She glistened in the struggle. Her eye was in to such an extent that she never looked his way. His hands lacked the ball, intensely moulding it but fixed—a sort of impotent force held out. Now she was tiring. The ball bounced too much. She was ready to flop but Uncle George was restless and laughing. And then the ball came up in a curve, not fast, wandering away as if in boredom from the bat that bossed it.

William moved, relaxed his hands, and had it fast. He spun on his heel: one sea horizon, one shore. It was enough to celebrate victory.

'No-ball,' said Uncle George. 'Good catch though.'

'It was,' he said. It was in his hands.

'Delivered from half way up the pitch?' Uncle George laughed. 'Wasn't it, Meg?'

'Mummy, you saw.'

'He's probably right,' said his mother. 'Not that I know about cricket.'

He handed her the ball. 'Bowled Goodyear, caught Goodyear.'

'Uncle George said no-ball,' she said gently.

'Mummy, when I was out, I went out. He's *out*.'

'Come on, Meg, get the over over.'

'Try again,' she said.

He looked at her. 'No, he's out.'

'Bill, it's only a game.'

'It's cricket,' he said. Magic word and last hope.

'Just a game. It's beach cricket anyway.'

'You didn't say anything when *I* was out.'

'Don't be tiresome, Billy.'

So that was it. He went on, knowing how loathsome his insistence was. 'You told *me* not to be "childish" and I went out. I gave the bat to *him* and I went out.'

'Oy,' said Uncle George. 'Umpire's decision is final.'

'You're out!' he screamed. 'I caught you out.'

The tall figure on the sand tossed his bat from one hold to the other. 'Do you want to stop the game?'

'Yes.' He was so overpowered. 'You don't know the rules.'

'I made them up, laddy.'

'Uncle George played for Essex.' His arm was touched. His mother. He broke. Sobs pumped from him and the dark shape of the blazer wobbled on the sand. Now he was defeated, but freed.

'*Cheat!*' The sea fractured in his eyes as he went towards it.

The sea had run round his feet, consoling. There was some splashing. Hubert had taken his hand but didn't look at him; they both looked out to sea. Then Hubert ran off, leaving his hand so close on itself and and on a grief made languid by the sea, so that his sobs came slower and washed him like a beach.

'I shouldn't worry about *him*.' Janet spoke casually, suspicious that he was still sniffing. Though it was colder now and no one, she noticed—remembering mothers—had reminded him to put on shirt or jumper. 'He's not the sort of person *to* worry about.' Friendliness was delightful and safe: to be involved, yet not—she knew she enjoyed it. Cousin Arthur had lapsed of course and was diminished. Things were different. The little ones had been agog for a minute or two, the grownups had carefully let it go. But she knew as well as he did that it still hung about. Janet half grasped the peculiar wisdom of being a between age, as he was too.

She suggested looking for an octopus. 'They're supposed to have them, tiny ones. Daddy says it's the Gulf Stream. Everything seems to be the Gulf Stream.'

'He's good at cricket.' William dutifully followed her round rockpools, sniffing.

'I happen to think cricket's rather stupid.'

'I don't know.'

'Well, if you don't know. They make a lot of it but it's only knocking a ball about.' She wondered he needed telling such things. 'I suppose you play it at school?'

'Not properly. We just knock a ball around.'

'There you are then. Octopus!'

They both crouched down, their faces dancing on a burnished sky. It took a lot of pointing out, of wheres and theres. At first she wasn't sure—it could have been seaweed. Small and trailing, it was like a cigarette-end in the lavatory pan. Janet giggled.

'I think I can see it,' he said.

'I'd pick it out if I dared. Perhaps they die if you do.'

'I will,' he said.

'I don't want death on your hands. It looks harmless. It looks like a cigarette in the lavatory.'

The word lingered on the pool. Cousin Arthur studied the surface with concentration. She was not sure he had seen the small tobacco-coloured thing.

'Does your father drop his ends down the toilet?' she asked, changing the word but not the subject. 'Ours is in constant hot water about it.'

'I don't know,' he said, sitting on his shanks, studying.

It seemed a bit colder than it was, bleaker. Cousin Arthur was difficult, perhaps tedious. Standing, she lost track of the octopus. Seeing it had been something. She was pleased to see her father stepping across rocks.

'What are you two up to?'

'Seeing a Monster of the Deep.'

'Let's have a look. What am I looking for?'

'Something with eight arms that squirts ink.'

'My children,' he said.

She smacked his familiar hairy arm. 'Very funny,' she said. It was, she thought. She slid her arm round his waist. Against him Sir Rommel was thin and so was William, poor Cousin Arthur. 'It was an octopus.'

'Hullo, Bill. Where is it?'

'It went behind a rock.'

'I'm not absolutely certain,' she said, 'he even saw it.'

'If there are no witnesses...' said her father. 'She sees snakes in the coal cellar, this one.'

Then it paraded round its pool for all to see. 'I told you so,' she fluted.

The way William said 'It's nice' told her he was seeing it for the first time. 'Sort of all watery.'

It moved, its tremulous grove of feet knowing the water as it went. His vision of it bettered and replaced hers of shredded tobacco. Though she had seen it first she had not seen it quite as he had, and she did not altogether like the realisation. On his haunches, her father made a soft rock to lean along and his springy hair a good chinrest. From that sunny spot she said: 'How long is Mr Straker staying?'

'She invariably wants to know everything.'

Being discussed was to her taste but she administered a good dig in his ribs. 'She is the cat next door.'

'Is it a baby one?' William felt impelled to ask a question, perhaps because Uncle Anstey was a teacher. It was odd to remember that fact.

'Between you and me I think it's a cuttlefish. Marine biology isn't my strong point.'

He felt no interest in identifying it. Enough to be there in the water, identifying itself. Water was all round him, running in and out and through him so that it became impossible to tell where he ended and water started, water which extending from himself held off the world outside like an unbreakable window filled with changing reflections.

Through which Uncle George waltzed with Tricia. He was

16

singing a fairly ancient hit about I'd like to get you on a slow boat to China and trailing the others with buckets and babies trying to keep up. As to what to say to him first since 'cheat', he hadn't thought. Easier to be submarine like the octopus which had moved from liquefied daylight into some unknowable vault to pry.

Uncle George announced: 'We've been climbing those stacks. I'm Mountain Goat, aren't I, Trish? Heard me yodel?'

'For pity's sake, George.' His mother had her share of baskets and clutter.

He yodelled or at least yoed. 'No echo,' he said. 'Not likely to be at sea-level. Your sister weighs a lot.'

William looked up quickly, leaving hiding to his proxy the octopus. It was an olive branch and he was willing, almost eager to take it. It was a mistake—Uncle George was talking to John Anstey and meant Janet lolling on her father's back.

'She's got grandad's bones,' said John.

Singing Waltzing Matilda, Uncle George peeled Janet off and danced away with her round the pool. It was marvellous how his feet found places to land. Caught in the grip of the blazer, she looked small and William remembered she was a child. Uncle George legged it seawards. His brass band played tiddley-om-pom-pom as he went out of earshot. The grown-ups were laughing. 'Petrified,'—Aunt Liz—. 'Talk about swept off her feet. She's been on for ages to have ballet lessons.'

Tricia was still dancing in the shallows of the pool. The arrival of Uncle George had got the octopus overlooked.

'He is a fool,' said his mother, apologising in general. He overheard and distrusted it. Was that what she felt?

When Uncle George came in to land, Janet held like a crucifix, motionless and stony-faced, he said: 'Thank you for the pleasure.'

He said: 'Eighty pounds of meat and bone,' patting Janet and then, with an owl-face at Tricia, 'Twice as heavy as you.'

'She's older. I'm only eight.'

'Perhaps she's got lead in her pants.'

His wink went too. Janet had pushed him. The splash was huge.

TWO

She had stopped crying but prolonged the aftertaste, as the sun was doing. It was a fitting state and right for a queen to be in, though she had not thought of her royalty or of Sir Rommel as such. It was more real and more luxuriant. The pullover, her favourite of vast and knobbly knit, was more comfortable than an embroidered cloak. It was cushioning her from the chiselled stones of this, her corner up on the farm wall.

The farm had more hiding places than she had ever seen; high and reached across the pigsty roof, this was the best. Janet kissed her wrist. One real tear, the last, made its way there and coursed its grain of salt into her mouth. Since the splash they had moved among torments. She smiled into her wrist exactly like a cat stretching itself. In their different ways everybody had had a go at her. She'd held out amazingly, until it had got too much.

After two days she was used to the farm which, except for the green-houses, was like a story-book farm; the fields were so small that they grazed the cows at the end of a lead. There below was a tethered cow. The setting sun made shadows like hills on its flanks. She tried to imagine that cows were like ground, like hills—and knew she was cribbing thin, unsatisfactory William's watery octopus. They were more like toys than hills, more like toy fields than fields in England.

'Jan!' Her father was standing near the pigsty, two blood-red suns on his face. She had the choice of either the righteousness of feelings kept going or ... not. It was easy enough to let friendliness come back.

He stood seen but unseeing in the yard. 'Janny!'

It was exactly as if he stood there with no one to see him. His isolation touched her. 'Here!'

'Time to hit the hay.' He crunched through old buckets. 'You ruminating?'

'That's right.' It was open to her to prolong anger as she had tears but that promised no pleasure. As usual her father left it open.

'Cows ruminate,' he said. 'Jump. I'll catch you.'

'Eighty pounds or whatever it was?'

'That doesn't still rankle, does it?'

'Oh no,' she said softly. 'Accused of being a liar and I don't know what.'

'I'm still not clear. Did you push him? I happened to be looking the other way.'

'You always are.' It was lying there to be said, not that she wanted to force a repeat of hours boiling like milk, over and then dry.

'Well, I'm not now. The truth matters, Jan.' He tried to pull himself up beside her but his arms changed his mind. 'I would like to know.'

'Why? Like a whodunnit, The Great Seaweed Mystery?'

'No. Truth is the only thing worth knowing.' He dusted his hands. 'That's weak. Truth's somehow special, the point of rest. It won't be taken down and used in evidence.'

'You mean you want to know for your own private satisfaction?' She liked him like this. They could spend a long time arguing what no one else in the family could see the point of.

'Not to mention the Principle of the thing?'

'If I pushed him?'

'Yes.'

'I gave him a helping hand. Assisted passage like going to Australia.'

'I wish you didn't sound so pleased about it.'

'I'm not—but I'm not not pleased either. I didn't do it for a reason, so don't ask me. Justice was done.' Her feckless elation somehow accorded with the sun, part of what the

lightfingered sun picked up as it went over the horizon. 'He's
so *conceited* and he got hold of me in his silly games. I thought
he wanted to make a splash.'

'I wish you hadn't, love.'

'Pray tell me why.'

'I can't, except to say that little girls don't push gentlemen into rockpools. But you know that already. The other
reason will have to keep.'

'The Great Uncle George Mystery.'

'Jump.'

She jumped and he caught her as he had for years. Instead
of going straight in they walked into one of the small fields.

'I hadn't noticed that barn,' she said.

'Shh. There's a pig trying to get to sleep.'

She looked in and saw a sack. 'It's a sack. A pig trying to
get to sleep!'

'So it is. Look at that window catching the sun.'

'It's iron gone rusty.'

'It's the reflection.'

'No, it's not.'

He went nearer. 'Well, I'll go to sea.'

'Really!' Two triumphs one after the other. 'At least snakes
in the coal cellar aren't pigs trying to go to sleep.'

'All right. So your poor old dad is cracking up.'

She took his hand through the darkening yard. The day
had been tiring; she knew that she would leave her book un-
opened under the pillow. 'It did look a bit like glass.' A sack
and rusty tin. Once, not long ago, she wouldn't have looked
twice—or else have believed him when she looked.

'Give a little hop and you come up with the waves.'

He clenched his teeth and hopped.

'Let it take you,' she said. 'You float if you let yourself.
You'll never learn just up to your knees.'

'I swallowed a bit.'

'That doesn't matter. Listen, Arthur, let me hold your
chest and you'll feel your feet floating.' She swam a few

scurried strokes. 'I learnt last year. It's easy, honestly. Once you let yourself. You've got to let yourself. The sea does it for you.'

His teeth were tight shut but she knew he was listening and taking in her words as well as sea-water. She sounded convincing and it was all true. The sea held, moved and caressed you. 'Ready?'

He offered himself, shivering, a victim.

'You're not scared, are you?'

'No.'

'I learnt in a swimming-bath and it's easier in the sea.'

'It's a bit deep.'

'Hold my hands and kick.'

Janet felt at least as competent as the swimming instructress at school, identical in fact with that tall and popular mistress.

He moored himself to her wrists and kicked his feet.

'That's the ticket.' Miss Leake's actual words. 'Relax.'

His clenched and whitening face bobbed on the sea's chopping-block and his feet threshed about.

'That's it,' she said when a seventh wave parted them, turned her upside down, burgled her breath and threw her up spitting.

The glittering points of the sea galloped to the beach with no sign of a head.

She panicked to find him but there was no way of telling where he had been and no chance he'd be there if she found it. Gaining the beach, she was ready to collapse into thoughts of Judgement: an eye for an eye, a Cousin Arthur for an Uncle George. Her father was reading the *News Chronicle* there had been so much trouble getting.

'I've lost Arthur—William—out there.'

'I've just seen him.'

'He's probably drowning.'

'He was in one piece when I saw him.'

'Are you sure?'

'He seemed all there.'

'You do it on purpose. You're not fit to be in charge of children. What was he doing?'

'Going up the cliff somewhere I think.'

'Just now?'

'Yes.'

'Right,' she said. 'And me out there swimming about, looking for his body.'

'I'll tell him off for you. Perhaps he'll go and drown himself. He probably will when he sees your face.'

'I don't think it's funny.'

She went on up the path, the gradient soon defeating any other exertions. He must have swept in on a wave. He could have let her know. Even have searched for her.

Now she had a vertical sea-view and a glimpse of the next bay with war-stuff sticking up. John had been full of some big gun left by the Germans but he was there with the others among a whole map of canals. William was the only one not there, but she could not see him on the clifftops either. Walking slowly, she was at a loss; whatever she had meant to say to him had evaporated on the ascent.

She was alone. The sea, the Gulf Stream, the fishy-eyed sea-gulls went on without her; she walked along the cliff path, alive, scuffing the sand, the small plants there, dusty and dumb but alive as well. The blue sky, cloudless, hung down its miles. Down from her a long way her father was reading his paper—the children filled buckets with the beach and the sea.

Sir Rommel faded here like a clifftop butterfly. Then she saw a wall up from the path, a little fort, a place to explore and anchor to. It was not hard to believe that she was the explorer discovering old ruins or the Queen arrived at the far side of the horizon, cast away on a desolate shore where the native tribes would provide a new people and a new recognition. She listened to the sea and brushed some fine sand from the leaves of a spiky plant which was laying siege to the wall. John knew all about forts, the round towers against Napoleon and the concrete places the Germans had built, places the grown-ups talked of seriously to each other and stopped talking of when you asked them. Gaschambers, according to John—gruesome bits of information were all he was good for. Grateful to her plimsolls, Janet climbed the wall. If not dangerous, it was tricky enough to give colour to her story when she got back. The twisted stems of the plant gave her handholds and the masonry pushed out by its roots let her feet rest as she went up. She aimed at an aperture made for a cannon. Gulls cried warning and disapproval as she scaled the rampart.

When she got there she heard Aunt Meg, perhaps because the word on the air just then was 'Janet', her own disavowed name. Aunt Meg's voice carried light and clear out from the gun place into the humming, booming heat of the sea-day. And Janet, who had mastered the height, who was precisely in control of her balanced body, balanced there in pure enjoyment—the sweat of climbing tart on her tongue, the situation of overhearing exactly like a story—even if it was only Aunt Meg.

'You can't expect children to act like adults, they don't.'

'You can expect them to act like well brought-up kids. I can. You're saying they normally push adults in the water, disrupt games of cricket and carry on in general like little Huns.'

She could hear matches—Uncle George's pipe. When a cloud of blue and smelly smoke puffed up it gave her more pleasure by proving her right than it did for him; at least the next thing he said was grumpier than ever. 'I find it bloody sickening, Margaret. Come all this way to be ragged by kids.'

'Janet isn't mine, George, and you know William's touchy. You can't expect him not to be. You didn't play beach-ball, did you?'

'I don't know what I did come for.'

'You remember Blackpool, I suppose.'

'There's been a war since then.'

'I'd like a go on the Big Dipper.'

Janet listened for more. She remembered Blackpool in connection with luminations; she recalled talk in the Infants about spies and passwords. But now the War was over—it was a puzzle.

She remained perfectly still, her mouth shaped exactly into the crook of her arm, enjoying the friendly savour of her own flesh. Her eyes were very close to the stone of the embrasure where various things normally too small to notice walked in the shadow of chisel marks on the outskirts of forests of lichen and moss half familiar to her from Nature Study. She had the unexpected thought that she was a spy—except that spies used their eyes and here were hers doing no more than Nature Study. She sniffed. The pipe had gone out and they had stopped talking. It was too risky to move though it needed only a small movement to look right down on them. Janet was being cautious, a spy. Her guess was that they had gone to sleep, something grown-ups were quite capable of, like her father's famous cat-naps on buses. She was beginning to tire of the position—deftly balanced spy—when she heard a groaning, grunting sound.

It sounded like a pig and she'd pictured one caught in a bramble before she knew that it wasn't. She had also remembered that sack and a little squeal of her own was only just trapped between her lips. It wasn't a pig. Janet knew that much about it. It was impossible to know quite what she did know about it. For the first time she could crank herself forward and take a peek.

The noise came and went. Uncle George bursting his blazer buttons! She grimaced at the sun. Really it was very odd being a spy, finding out without being found out. She wanted to look and moved her head forward but the preceding shadow would drop into the fort before she could see. So that was that; she could climb down the wall with nothing more to avoid disturbing than loose stones.

On the path she looked up at the rampart with a new idea of its height and a measured knowledge of the place. But she was tired of the scenery, these cliffs, this sea.

Stones on the path were few. She picked up a big one, threw

it and it disappeared insignificantly between the seagulls' sky-scrapers of air.

He could not doubt the great extent of his failure. The misery of fear ran from him faster than seawater; he shivered in the sun. He'd come ashore further along than the encampment of folding chair, children and thermos flasks. This was the bit of coast famous for its bays and he had landed at the point between theirs and the next. Either could be walked into because the tide was low. He went into the next which was small, a cove not a bay. He was the only person there and walked round it. There were caves so cold that they cured his shaking and his teeth. They had the coldness of the earth and the sun had never lit them.

William rolled down his trunks; the sea had made him white and shrinking. His warm urine splashed back on his feet but he didn't mind it. In this cave you could think. He had waded out with Janet and suddenly though the bottom had been firm, smooth and not too far down there had been no bottom and she had changed from the girl he knew into pieces—a voice, colours, hands. He'd had to fight simply to be ordinary and go through with it. And he was a failure—afraid of the water. Now that it was over he could think of the sea without agitation. He had always liked the water and yesterday—the beautiful little octopus. Jolly nearly, he had felt himself swimming with it.

The rocky point was swirling now. Technically he was cut off : a boy needing rescue, pulled up the front pages of newspapers by ropes. But the sea was only knee-deep and he could walk it with no trouble, no qualms, except that he had not yet explored the cove and at the back of his mind already there was the cliff. He stared into the miniature depths of several rockpools, perhaps hoping to see some other creature demonstrating how easy it was, being alive.

That push Janet had given Uncle George, had it frightened him? He didn't believe it. She had just done it, a little shove which he reproduced against the cliff. Everyone had laughed, he had himself, as if to please Uncle George—pleased to be able to. But he had arisen in anger, dripping and slipping. His mother had laughed, they had both laughed. Then all that talk and the car full of questions. He had not called her Eleanour but if you called people by names that weren't real *you* gave the names. He tried to invent one. Joan of Arc came but that wasn't much good—she'd been burnt at the stake. What he remembered was a name his father had given him. It was Binny and there was a big long field with buttercups and daisies and it was before he was away all the time.

He came to the cliff and looked at what he'd chosen. It wasn't too bad. At first a whole lot of slabs and boulders made outsized steps. The speed you could go at over rocks was surprising: you had to keep moving and think ahead of your feet. Then it was easier than walking up a hill where you plodded and needed no brain.

On the cliff it was different but still satisfying. Here he had to find out how to go up the vertical, inventing a rule to keep three firm anchors and never have more than one foot or hand looking for a place. The main difference was time, being slow not quick. Once he seemed stuck and had to break his own rule—then it was luck that kept him on. Half way up his feet skidded on a down-sloping ledge covered with gravel: that was a dance and he got out of the spot in an ecstasy of fear. This was more dangerous than the sea. William knew he'd get up and not lie at the bottom of a newspaper page, one cutting his mother wouldn't collect. Completely new to him came the idea that his mother could be reached if he broke a leg, say, instead of his neck. She would not happen to be having to talk to Uncle George. But it was like someone else's idea, something you read. He had no intention of falling. Yet he knew that even when he came over the top he would remain a sea-failure.

When he did, everyone was waiting for him. Adult voices trailed down half heard, for the last bit was best, hardest, just right to end with. Scraps of unnecessary advice, mostly to do with not rushing, were aimed down the cliff. It amused him because it was so much like grown-ups to fancy they were in charge; according to them their last minute words were getting him up the cliff.

He stood there, a small boy with scraped knees. It was one of the transformations people did to you. Then his mother hugged him as she hadn't for a long time, so hard it hurt his breastbone.

THREE

The ground was dusty. Janet went up the lane lackadaisically. One of the things about the farm was the slackening of bed-time. Parents were quite grateful if you went out for a bit, because they had to pack the little ones one by one off to the Land of Nod. The baby. Mark, who was a little devil. Hubert —she guiltily remembered a promise to tell him stories. John who liked sleep more than anything. By that time she the sensible, she the firstborn, was forgotten. It was a pity there was hardly anything to do in this freedom of the dusk. Just wander round the farm. Sometimes, as now, it seemed to Janet that life was limitless and featureless like the sea. Then she would feel the beginnings of restlessness, as if she would run herself into the ground merely to get somewhere definite.

The lane skirted a quarry, which was where the farm buildings had come from, according to Mr Chauvel. 'Before your time,' he'd said. 'Before mine. Hundreds of years, what they call centuries.' Grown-ups without children interested her—they had ideas about what you knew at your particular age. Mr Chauvel talked to her and to Hubert in the same way. He was being kind. She, who had lived through centuries!

Then she saw Cousin Arthur by the quarry. She had thought of him as being in bed, if she had thought of him at all. But he was staring into the dark, squarish pan of water, still up like her at the day's loose end. He didn't shift his eyes when she stood beside him. Partly because of the dusk he seemed only half there. She resolved to say nothing, letting him speak first: it was artificial, something to do almost, like counting telegraph poles. Let him say nothing at all. In a minute though she had posted a stone into the water. It spoke for her.

Plop.

'It must be deep,' he said.

'Mr Chauvel said it's where they got the bricks for the house.'

'Stones. Bricks are baked out of clay.'

'That's what I meant.'

'They call them brickfields where they do it. There's an old one near us.'

'That's funny,' she admitted. 'Like a brickfarm and brick-stacks and cows dropping bricks. Have you seen Mr Chauvel milking?'

'Yes,' he said. There was enough reticence in that for her to prod in the half-dark past what concerned her, just to do it.

'Merrily, merrily will I live now,
Under the blossom that hangs on the cow.'

It was a version of a song at school and she sang it softly, sweetly into the quarry. 'One of our songs,' she said. 'Do you have it at your school?'

'No.'

'We've changed the words. It should be "bough" like on a tree.'

'Yes,' he said.

'It's funny,' she said, realising. 'They call cows "Blossom"; it's one of the names for cows.'

'It puts you off milk,' he said, 'seeing it come out like that.'

'Does it?' She leaned forward on the rail, stretching quite a long way over to see if she could see herself looking up again from the quarry's dark mirror. He told her to steady on. She could not see beyond the dusty plants. 'You could climb down and rescue me.'

'I don't know. That cliff wasn't so bad as it looked. This is harder.'

Janet did not care for his practicalities but she was shivering at the thought of swimming round and round that sheer pool with nowhere to climb out. She stood back from the rail, still feeling stretched—she was as tall as the trees the rooks were settling in.

'There's nothing wrong with where milk comes from, is there?' From the depths where the farm had come from to the tops with nests, she looped round Cousin Arthur to note details like a flannel shirt and hair which had been brushed.

'I tried to do it. It's sort of rubbery.'

She had only watched. 'Did Mr Chauvel let you?'

'I asked.'

'Really?' Janet had not even thought of asking. There was Mr Chauvel and the cow swishing its tassel and the milk shushing into a bucket. He had asked and discovered what it was really like; she who could take in time and space without thinking did not know as much.

'It's late now,' he said. 'There are loads of bats.'

'Bats?'

'I know where they hang around in the daytime. They do hang around.' He laughed. 'You know: upside-down.'

'Like umbrellas.'

'Bit like that.'

'You're making it up,' she said. The whole place was known to her, wholly, and not once had she seen a bat.

'I see well in the dark. If you look you'll see them flying. They fly soft and it's sort of sonic. Like radar.'

'I don't know if I want to.'

'I think they hibernate.'

'I hope they are,' she said. 'They go for your hair if you're a girl. Yours is so neat you'd be all right but mine's frizzly from swimming.'

'Mum brushed it. She thinks I'm in bed.'

'Does she? They let me stay up late if I want to. On holiday anyway. Won't Aunty Meg be cross if she finds you out?'

'She won't,' he said. 'Not unless she's got radar. She's gone to the town.'

'St Peter Port?'

'We have to go to bed as early as at home. Earlier really. I had an illness last year. It's gone now.'

31

'Did you go to hospital?' The whole unknownness of his life struck her: he was a sort of cousin but, apart from a picnic in a forest in the story-book of her early memories, Christmas cards and featuring from time to time in her mother's reports of letters, he was unknown—just a relation and slightly boring because a relation. Now to be interested in him (and there was no one else) made him a quarry to get things out of.

'I was in for eleven days.'

'That's ages.'

'We got good food.'

'Extra eggs?'

'The miners gave up their ration or something for the children in hospital.'

'Egg miners. Careful with that pick!'

'The matron was awful. Even the Sisters were afraid of her.'

'We're never ill.' It was true—medicine bottles were not a feature of the Anstey household. Suddenly it seemed unfair. Everything at home was so ordinary, so known. 'What are Sisters? I mean I know they're nurses and all that.'

'They're in charge of the wards and they have Night Sisters. You don't see those unless you wake up, but they're always there.'

'It sounds all right. Are they nice?'

'Some are. We had a very nice one called Sister Kerr.'

'What are Matrons?'

'Matrons are in charge. There's only one usually. They're very important and tell the doctors what to do.'

Janet said: 'I bet they wouldn't tell ours.' Known as Uncle Peter, theirs had dropped in as long as she could remember to talk to her father and sprinkle pipe-ash. The thought wafted her back to the afternoon and smelling out 'Uncle George'. 'He says if everyone was like us he'd be out of a job. I don't think I know anyone who's been in hospital.' She had rushed on into confession.

'It was for observation,' he said.

Janet hummed agreement. She wasn't going to ask about *that*. 'Show us these bats.'

'They won't be there now. They come out when it gets dark. If we don't move we ought to see them in flight.'

'My hair.'

'You and your hair,' he said.

'I should think so.' It was odd: truly she didn't mind the risk. They were both aware of playing adults.

'I tell you what. Tie a handkerchief over it. It's a big one of dad's and it's clean.'

'Thanks.' It came out of his pocket, a neatly laundered sandwich. She knotted the corners as her father did to keep the sun off little ones' heads. 'It's funny having a father's handkerchief but not having a father.'

'I have got a father.'

'Why isn't he here then?' She combed with her hand, then stowed her hair away. 'Unless you don't want to talk about it.'

William threw a stone he had into the darker-than-ever quarry. His skidded on the rock, barked and clopped. Above, in their nests, the rooks were silent. It was the last breath of day, almost night.

'These bats,' said Janet, changing the subject, cheaply victorious.

'It's difficult to talk about it.' He had faded to a dot, not even dots for knees; he had long trousers on, she'd noticed.

'You'd rather not,' she said with a note of discretion caught from grown-up conversations. But quite suddenly in the night she was attuned to a web as sonic as anything the bats did, as full of mysterious flight.

'It's a mystery,' he said with a stunning sadness. 'Dad was away a lot in the War. When I see him it's usually in cafés. You know, I wait and then he comes in and buys me buns.'

'A sort of rendezvous?'

'A bit like that. It was in the Natural History Museum in London. Under the whale.'

'Does he seem all right?'

33

'Quiet,' said William. 'He smokes cigarettes and tells me things.'

Janet tried hard to picture the rendezvous—Cousin Arthur, hair brushed, his mysterious father—her uncle—always in cloud like Ben Nevis when they had lived two months in Scotland. The whale.

'What's the whale like?'

'It's huge. He's not real, made of plaster and sort of blue. You can tell it's plaster because there's bits fallen off. The museum's not open properly. It's because of the War. It's tremendously long and the basic design is the same as a submarine.'

'Did he tell you that?'

'He was in the Navy.'

'The Silent Service,' said Janet, adding anchors, crowns and other frippery of consequence to Cousin Arthur's father. 'If we don't get in there'll be panic-stations.'

As they went through the yard he touched her arm. 'Look, Eleanour.'

The name puzzled her for an instant. 'Bats?'

'Yes.'

She felt the night electric and crammed with sounds inaudible to normal hearing; but saw nothing with her ordinary sight.

A bit of wind was up and beginning to tear white stuffing out of the blueness of the sky which had seemed set for good.

It grated the leaves of the few old palm trees, rattled the ratlines of the schooner in the inner harbour and made flesh brisk. It had been a morning in the town for the mothers' benefit. They had given expert reports on what the shops had to offer and because of some difference of rationing they were pleased.

William sat on the wall with Janet, eating a meagre toffee-apple. Ice-cream had been rumoured and the mothers were off on a cold scent, taking the hordes of small ones with them and John with his birthday money and wish for a boat and

34

Tricia because she liked shops. Which left the two of them on the harbour wall. Expert in cigarette cards, he told her it was a schooner.

'It's nice. I like sailing boats.'

'They went round Cape Horn. That's the worst place in the world.'

'I think Manchester is. Have you been?'

William shook his head and dropped his toffee-apple—a stroke of luck, for he preferred not finishing it.

'We have been around,' she said. 'Aren't these awful apples? I suppose that's why they bake them in this stuff.'

He watched her strong and expert teeth dealing with the spiked fruit. A flap of hair smothered her face at one moment and then lifted from her forehead. He could have wished for her as a sister. And then she mentioned Tricia. 'She's never eaten three.'

'She's rather greedy.' He felt no betrayal in the announcement. 'Uncle George likes spoiling her.'

'He's still looking at that naval boat. He's been there ages.'

Down the quay the light shimmered on shipping and blared from the sides of fortifications, old stone supplemented by Nazi concrete: colours danced like bunting. Furtively William pressed the underlids of his eyes to clarify the picture but no Uncle George came into focus. Unknown to anyone, he was short-sighted, though he got through except for certain occasions such as spying at a distance in the jostling light.

'Uncle George is mysterious as well,' she said, swinging legs. 'It might be a coincidence. Do you think he's planning something?'

'What?'

'I don't know. Mr Chauvel said the Germans had hidden gold on the island. He said it was to pay for the invasion of England.'

William rubbed up his memories of *Treasure Island* which Mr Henderson had read in four hundred instalments. The palm trees were not up to it—doubloons unlikely.

35

'He's going tomorrow.'

'Not stopping the holiday?'

When William told her he'd come over to do some business with his mother, she seemed to titter—the stray wisp of a giggle, then sat on her hands. 'That's rather interesting,' she said at last. 'Isn't it hot with all that cloth round your legs?'

'You have to fold them up at night to keep the crease.'

'John's mad about them. It's his latest thing. You'd think long trousers were the most super-dooper thing on earth.'

'They're jolly comfortable,' he said. Chiefly they had the advantage of covering more of him up. He remembered his excitement when his mother had suddenly unwrapped them. She'd said he was her man; and Tricia's jealousy carrying so far that she had been offered a pair of her own.

'I dare say he's on about them this very minute.'

'Oughtn't we to go and find them? They might be looking for us.'

'No, Arthur dear— Uncle George is coming. It might look a little obvious.'

William was too pleased with what she had called him to be nervous. More mysterious than German gold, she tidied her face of hair and folded her arms.

Each day Uncle George had changed. The blazer had given way to a white tropical jacket with enough button-down pockets to make even Tricia think of abandoning a sweet-hunt. Today that had gone too and Uncle George came down the harbour in a short-sleeved sports shirt. On his face he had black R.A.F. sun spectacles and on his feet sandals from Egypt with just a noose for the big toe. They had had the history of these miracles at breakfast. The fishermen, who had not, eyed him as they might a bright stray in their nets, something too out of the run of things to take seriously.

'Hullo, you two.'

The blazer and the tropical jacket had disguised the heaviness of his stomach; the sports shirt didn't.

'Hullo,' said Janet. 'We thought we'd lost you.'

Uncle George laughed. 'You wanted to, did you?'

'Not particularly.'

William in his cowardice hoped she was his match. To be on the wall was an advantage of height. The black glasses, though they made it easier for you to look at him, presented two small yourselfs trapped in his red face.

'Just in general, eh? Nice day for a swim. If you've got a costume of course.'

'We don't happen to,' said Janet. 'And the harbour's not the best place, I'd say.'

'I could tell you somewhere else that wasn't.'

'That incident's closed.' Janet sat on her hands again.

Uncle George roared. 'She takes the biscuit, doesn't she, William?'

'Yes,' he said, not sure what it meant, sure only of his old confusion.

'If you two want a shufty round a real, genuine Motor Torpedo Boat I might be able to fix it. The lieutenant's an old friend. Never met before, but we were both on D Day. Like to?'

'Yes.' Carter's uncle was an admiral and Carter, according to himself, had been on a submarine.

'It would be very nice but we were told to wait here.'

'That won't matter,' said Uncle George. 'The chance doesn't come every day. This boat sails at midnight. Which by the way is probably confidential. She won't be here tomorrow.'

'We told them we'd wait.'

'Hard-hearted little miss, isn't she, Bill? All we want is a quick little reccee.'

'Arthur can go with you but I'm waiting.'

'Eleanour's probably right.' William had sat upon his own hands. Weakness, weakness.

'Who's Eleanour?'

'I am,' she said, relieving him of what he could not do. 'Occasionally.'

'And Bill's Arthur?'

'Sometimes.'

'You kids! Had me worried there. More names and so

many kids already it's hard to tell tother from which.'

'We can.'

'I'm sure you can. You've a great future, girly, whatever they call you. Any objections to photographs? I've got here one of the more acceptable presents from Hitler.' He undid leather. 'It's a genuine pre-war Leica. Say "Käser", that's cheese in German. Smile when you see the dicky bird and I shan't walk backwards into the dock, even for laughs. Hold it.'

They held it. William tried to get his face in order for the record. It was like being a hollowed turnip from his side of the smile. On snaps it ranged from tragedy through shades of melancholia and up to heights of deadpan.

'You'll crack the lens. Can't you sit a bit closer? Pretend you're honeymooners.'

They could scarcely credit his bad taste, edging towards each other and deploying mutual fenders of embarrassed disbelief.

'Put your arm round!' Three dark and glassy eyes maintained the scrutiny.

'For heaven's sake,' said Janet, convict-fashion from the corner of her mouth, 'let's get it over with.'

His apologetic hand rested on the red flowers of her waist. He hung between that dead contact and his guttering turnip smile whilst the flashing eyes adjusted themselves, behind them dark cavities about to take them in.

'Snapshot of the century. I'll have another squint at that MTB by myself then. The chap mentioned a wardroom and I feel a bit groggy.'

William found his hand on Janet's dress. He took it back. She sighed.

'You had to call me Eleanour,' she said. 'In front of *him*.'

'You said "Arthur" first. You told me to call you that.'

She ignored him. Instead, she practised lying flat out in a straight line, her legs one side of the wall with feet flattened and her arms stretched above her horizontal head. Only her hair hung down.

'It's a bit much,' he said. 'Telling me to call you that and then telling me off when I do.'

'It's not important.' She sounded relaxed, far more than she looked. 'What's more important is what Uncle George is up to. Can you do this?'

He tried but his head felt giddy half way. A boy in hospital had fallen on his head off a garage, jarring his neckbones. She was in danger of doing the same thing. He said: 'Your head's the heaviest part of your body.' But didn't add that she was showing her knickers.

'I know that.' She swung back to sitting effort, on an invisible trapeze. 'It's the first thing they teach you in swimming.' Just as gracefully she was on her feet—they were strong and straight-toed, not like his hammers and sickles. Decyphering the salty distance, she said: 'Now he's going *on* the boat. Can he swim?'

'I don't know anything about him.'

'It might be important. *And* I can see the others.'

People near the buses resisted eye-squeezing. There were the old palms champing their leaves. Beyond that, detail was scarce.

The day was one of those, something ajar in it. Maybe the wind took the edge off holidaying. There had been an attempt at the beach but for one reason or another no one had enjoyed it. They went to a small bay, one of the best they had been saving on Mr Chauvel's advice 'For a rainy day'—one of her father's witty jokes. Somehow they had tried it now, too soon—and it hadn't worked. The famous steps leading to its postcard sands had been too many—buckets dropped, babies grazed, wasps beaten off. The wind belted round the beach like a dog off its lead. Almost before they had time to stagger at the thought they were on the way up, trailing, winded and with only the promise of salad to keep them going.

Salad over, children were told to lose themselves. Mr Chauvel, far from being put out at the unexpected midday return, seemed happy to have children under his feet, calves under his arms, rabbits in his pocket. Noonday welter of growing flesh; farmer in his element. Seeing Tricia safely attached, Janet slipped off to their room. With Tricia in it she had never really taken possession. Propping open its atticky window, she prepared to do so.

'The younger girl's shoes lay in hapless confusion,' she announced. Gymshoes, vests and worse were pushed back to Tricia's bed, the one with a curtain which she had bagged by being first in (by two minutes). Janet remembered being envious of that bed three days ago when Sir Rommel had guarded the door of the chamber with a battleaxe. Now she was more conscious of its tired-looking mattress—and of the jumble on top. The curtain drew, shedding a faint mustiness. The rest of the room was bright with white paint and it was a pity the new wash-hand basin was yellow. At the time the Queen had not been much impressed by this feature, though to everybody else it had been a great wonder. Royalty did not wash and Sir Rommel had never been unarmoured in the sight of his sovereign. It was sheer luxury simply to flop on her own divan bed and study from there the washbasin, the patch of mirrored sky and the jug and ewer. Plaster was still drying round the pipes and the water-set had lingered on in case the newcomer failed.

She'd pushed the drawer shut with her foot and remembered her father's awful joke about drawers of wood and ewers of water before she got to asking herself why it was open at all. In it everything was as much in order as before but conviction grew that the drawer itself had been left closed. Numerous small incidents were flocking round with nothing to stick to. Back on the bed, she resolved to think it through. Fearsome concentration got her knees on the pillow, clamping her ears. Sherlock Holmes fell to the floor, not impressed.

She was friendly with herself but restless. Down from the window the whole farmyard was displayed: Hubert held aloft to some interesting hole by Mr Chauvel, John struggling with a wheelbarrow far too heavy for him and Cousin

Arthur visible as well, sitting in her special corner, chin on knees, shorts on.

As she spied through the window—seeing people who could not see each other—the restlessness increased. Somehow the day was untidy, as full of oddments as the drawers in the kitchen at home—cottonreels, envelopes, bits of dead clocks, things whose use no one knew but whose usefulness was taken on trust; a pair of absolutely incredible paper shoes from mummy's wedding-cake. Room though for emptiness as well.

She decided to wash her hair. People washed their hair at basins as well as in the bath—Lana Turner had in that film. You filled the basin and dipped in your head like a brush. Soon it was clearly drastic enough and what she'd needed. The water ran down you, given half a chance, so you had to hang like a tulip. Hair's soapy coils wound oddly under her fingers. Normally—always—her mother did it for her. When she stopped dripping she took a look. Odd Eleanour— shorn queen! It looked like no one she knew—a pixie, and so young! not even twelve.

It was just the moment for Tricia to come in.

'Where are my things?'

Janet rinsed the basin and plugged it. 'If you mean your dirty clothes,' she said, trying to sound like Miss Leake, 'I put them on your bed.'

'You oughtn't.'

'No. *You* ought.' Janet registered the cleverness of that without triumph. She wanted the youngness of the other girl to erase the pixie in the mirror, but it hadn't. At present Tricia looked a hundred years old.

'What are you doing that for?'

'I'm washing my hair.'

'They aren't entering you in the Show, are they?'

'The Show's been decided, has it?'

'Yes! And there's pony rides.'

Janet regretted her lordly tone and wondered if Tricia wasn't all right after all. She was three years younger but per- haps they could be friends. In a way it was immensely desirable to be the friend of someone younger, more comfortable than with someone your own age. Tricia though was more likely to be a problem than William. He wasn't satisfactory but she liked him more. The girl was unguaranteed.

'I might go.' Her face still mizzled over with water, she identified the towel in her hand as one of the awful Goodyear ones and grabbed her own.

'Can you ride?'

'A bit,' she said. It didn't matter that it was Eleanour who rode so well, flanked by gleaming escort through forests dripping darkness. In her other capacity she had been on a donkey before the War, her mother said.

'My Uncle George has to go back. He won't be here after tomorrow. He came all the way to see me.'

'Did he say so?' Her hair was miraculously almost dry. 'It's like an oven in here,' she said, brushing it. 'You can't always believe what people say,' she said, imagining a hairpin between her teeth. Lana Turner had just such a conversation round a hairpin, except with Gregory Peck or someone.

'Me and mummy then.'

'And Cousin Arthur?' A few more brush-strokes and she'd take a look.

'Who?' It sounded as rude as what instead of pardon. Tricia lacked all grace.

'Your brother William.'

'He's *useless*. He was useless with cricket and useless when Uncle George fell in. We're ashamed of him. He must be as old as you.'

'A few months difference.' She looked and was pleasantly surprised. If not Lana Turner, the face was no longer a pixie's.

'I'm going down. They'll be ready soon, so don't take ages.'

'Yes, you run along,' said Miss Leake.

Her hair hung straight and quite long. She closed the door without too much argument with the doorpost. On inspection her shirt ranked with Tricia's and went out of sight into one of the drawers. In its place she chose the best

42

white shirt, the one which was almost a blouse and her Speech Day skirt. Newly dressed in the mirror her hands stayed on her chest prefiguring the coming transformation. She was caught a moment, puzzling. Did she want it or didn't she? She didn't know what she wanted and the line so appropriate from mouths fitted with hairpins or cigarettes—'That is the story of my life,' generated the peculiar satisfaction of a smile in private.

'You're quite right, my dear,' she said, scooping up a previously unseen garment and dropping it behind the curtain. To go at midnight would be to have gone tomorrow. The book she placed back under her pillow. The window she closed: it was all or nothing, having no peg to stay it on. Outside no one was to be seen. Her particular niche of the wall was empty. The hooter of the hired car hooted from the front.

They were all amazed by the size of the Show, its variety. Between the trees of heavy summer there was every sort of sideshow, every sort of beast, thousands of people. The wind had died out of the day. This was inland if such a small island had one. The sea felt counties away.

Uncle George gave William the resumed blazer to hold and rolled up his sleeves. It was bigger than an overcoat and weighted with the things of Uncle George—wallets and keys, pipes and unknowns. In his hands it jangled faintly, heavy with the man's artillery. The Try-Your-Strength proprietor said: 'Ring the bell for a prize your madam can choose.'

'We could just do with a seashell bouquet.'

She was siding with him perhaps, for it had been Uncle George's idea to stop; the others had all gone on; she had objected: 'We all know how strong you are.'

'Tricia might like one,' he said.

'We'll make one,' she said with a quick look. 'Instead of spending time here.'

'We're here now, Meg. May as well enjoy it.'

43

'You will.'

'Feel those.'

Biceps swelled under his nose. 'Me?' He didn't want to do the wrong thing, be stupid, displease them.

Uncle George gave one of his bellows. 'Did you think I meant your mother?'

'Are you doing this or not?'

His hand lay on the swelling whiteness—tendons stood out in the brown forearm. 'Feel.'

As he gripped harder, William's hand conjured the cricket ball.

'Drinking arm.' Uncle George winked.

'For heaven's sake! Give me that.' His mother took the blazer, which had trailed in the dust. 'I don't see why you should hold it,' she said, putting an unconvincing arm round his shoulders. The strength machine was worked by banging a peg with a mallet. Something would shoot upwards to a level marked in pounds on one side, with little sayings on the other. 'Apply for Wheelchair.' 'Okay—for ninety.' 'Mr Hercules.'

The first whack—simply enormous—got the flying gleam only to 'Keep trying.' Repeated blows sent it higher, in sight of the summit before it fell back. Uncle George tried getting it on one side, then the other; he tried short forearm chops and Catherine-wheel swings. That terrible thing, a crowd, began to gather. 'For God's sake, George.' Her arm withdrew, she bundled the blazer. Dark patches were growing under the arms of Uncle George's shirt. He said: 'It's a swizzle.'

'You're past it.' His mother laughed, a sort of dead amusement.

'I'm all right.' One of his brown hands stroked the white muscle. 'Wouldn't you say, Bill?'

It was a real question coming from Uncle George, a surprising plea for support.

'It might get stuck,' he said.

'Two shillings.' It was astounding how the strength machine man had changed: friendly at first, now almost cross.

44

Uncle George told him off. 'Your bloody machine's been fixed.'

'You calling me, mister?'

'It's a well-known fact you make sure you win.'

'You blaming me for *that*?' The man touched Uncle George's stomach and drew a few giggles from the crowd. 'It'll be me who eats his breakfast next. I make a packet, I'm on the fat of the land. Let me show you.' He stretched his trousers out round his waist. 'I'm lost in here like a mouse in a cathedral.' It was like a clown's act; with red paint and powder he could have been a clown. Some of the crowd had gone but those left, rough ones, wanted entertainment free and at someone else's expense. William, standing next to his mother with nothing to hold, felt the smaller crowd working on the little man: his slivers of eyes were busy thinking. Uncle George holding the mallet like a cricket bat was going to be out this time. Yet, instead of pleasure, William felt embarrassment—cowardly on Uncle George's behalf in that sea of people, as if some terrible thing would happen to him as well. 'I tell you what—I'll make a sportsman's offer. If any one of you gents can bang the ring-a-ding this gent will hand over his two bob to the stronger chap. If not, it's quits all round. Can I say fairer than that?' He couldn't, to go by the noises of the growing crowd. Someone took the mallet from Uncle George.

He slipped off, telling his mother something she didn't hear. Going to see the cows was what he said. If he could get to that tent before the bell rang, that tree ... He did, and turned a corner. Now that he was free in it the crowd was bearable and even interesting. He picked out the boys and some of the girls of his own age. Especially the boys. Some were free, local and scruffy, these were glimpsed going under tents or up trees. Mostly they were in tow, hair smarmed, wrists manacled and something so familiar in their glances— the shame of being anchored to fathers and aunts—that superimposed level which stopped you doing anything and was busy and meaningless overhead.

Having passed the tent and the tree without hearing the bell he had become free and wouldn't hear it now. Best if it got stuck and the man apologized, shook hands, gave his mother a prize. He had left her and the situation he had left her in was too terrible to think about. His own action was easier because more clear and definite, walking off, like climbing a cliff—definite. If you thought out problems, even your own actions, you could solve them. Being caught at the strength machine had been an accident—a few yards nearer Uncle Anstey and he would have gone on with them. Holding the blazer had been no help—though she had taken that over. Being there made it all worse, worse for her. Like Captain Oates. For he did think of her, suffer for her. Tears attacked him like a wasp. He did not know how he had arrived at them. They parted on the Lost Children tent. No lost children in that green shade. It was a white tent, a toy soldiers' tent— white canvas swelled like biceps in Uncle George's arm. Why was his father away always?

'You need jodhpurs really. Have another go.' The lady held the horse's jingling head and smiled a kind of high-bred encouragement. She'd ridden up herself on a huge black animal. 'Face the tail and heave-ho.'

Janet held the saddle and tried to get her leg up and over. She nearly did.

'Let me show you.' The lady arched a long clad leg and was on. 'Press down with the foot and put rhythm into it. Do everything with rhythm, see?'

Janet nodded, learning.

'Now look at my knees, lightly pressing here. Look at my sit.'

Not sure where to look, Janet observed the perfectly white, bulging blouse, the riding hat sitting on almost blonde curls.

'Oh, and see the way I hold the reins, looped firm but not forcing. It's taken me eight years. Started about your age.' The lady seemed to recognise that too much perfection could

46

be discouraging. Janet had no doubts about her perfection. There was more of the goddess than queen about her. You could imagine her riding her life as easily as a horse—a total mistress. And here she was spending far more concern than a shilling charity ride required. This time she did it, with rhythm. Her knees bristled with the horse's hairy hide. She straightened her speech-day skirt, sat straight in her de-valued blouse and remembered to get the reins right, firm but not forcing. In front of her the animal twitched his ears and jangled iron-ware in his mouth.

'Bravo. We'll make a horsewoman of you yet.' Janet flashed a grateful smile. 'The walk's easy, so is the gallop actually. But the trot smacks you about the backside.'

That was odd but, Janet felt, allowable. Goddess leading, they moved. 'Which is this?' Janet had been brought up to take an intelligent interest.

'Walk.'

'How do you get them to trot?'

'My, I was right. We'll walk round first. You urge with the heels. You pull on the reins to reduce speed.'

'And say "Whoa".'

'Not necessary. A good horsewoman is part of the beast.'

'He seems a nice horse.'

'She's a pony.'

'Oh.'

'Never mind—you're doing fine.'

'Thank you.'

They rounded the arena. Beneath her the crowd looked on. There, anxiously expectant, the queue. Tricia somehow headed it. But she was right—the lady was taking far more than a perfunctory interest.

'This time she's all yours. Remember—heels to make her go, heels and she'll trot. Rhythm. Up and down.'

A buffeting lollop brought them to the shade of a large tree. In the dapple of it the she-pony stopped to pluck grass.

'Gee up.' A shifty glance, no goddess. 'Gee up!' Janet tugged at the reins and with a noise like vanishing bathwater

47

up came the jingling head and they were off. Every movement nearly flung her; exactly when the saddle came up she was descending. But instinct or Miss Leake told her to relax and amazingly the cobblestone juddering turned into a sort of smoothness. At the end of the field she reined in quite naturally, thumped with one foot and the beast came round. Ahead the great tree stood on its island of shadow. She seemed to get there by thought, horsepowered heels applied without thinking. The pony stooped to finish the tuft. 'Good boy.' She patted the neck, remembering it was a girl. Heel, reins, turn; they covered the same ground. She was aware of the achievement, aware too of its inspiration ... whom she saw talking to a young man. As the finishing touch she drew up right near them, patting the animal's neck again and consciously curbing bigheadedness, open demands for the accolade.

The goddess was altered, though it took her time to see it. For one thing she was prinking her nearly golden hair with a fussy hand and for another she was fingering her white shirt into the waistband of her jodhpurs.

The young man, tall, red-faced and with yellow eyebrows was licking an ice.

'There she is,' said the lady. 'I've a whole tribe more to get through, Nigel. Charity, you know, is pretty tedious.'

The big young man snorted and the goddess giggled. '*Really*,' she said in pointless emphasis.

'Jimmy thinks so. I'd lay a fiver on it.' Snort.

'You *bad* boy.' Giggle. Snortle.

Janet slid quietly down the horse's flank and walked away.

'Hi, I say.' The goddess pursued her.

'What?'

'Have I had your shilling?'

'Daddy paid it.' She walked away again. She was hurt of course and she refused to look back. Under the tree she pulled a handful of grass by the roots. At least the pony had not betrayed her. She flung it away. The lady *had* been interested. It was that Nigel who had interfered; by turning up he had stupefied the goddess. And it was obvious, that was the

48

awful thing! Stuffing in her shirt and giggling when on the horse she had been so superb. Janet decided not to go on feeling hurt; instead she began to marvel. Did the change do that much to you, put you out of your mind over someone so obviously boring as Nigel with his yellow eyebrows? It was the fate of being a girl that you could not guess far ahead. Despite her mother's announcements, she had never objected to being one: she possessed too many brothers. John, it was quite obvious what he'd turn out to be; long trousers, a pipe, a moustache even—John just the same. Her case was different: a sort of cliff you dropped over, a sort of horizon you could not see beyond.

So, instead of being jolted into the hurts of childhood she had come through. A victory, a series of them. It had not taken Eleanour eight years to master riding, nor eight minutes. Restlessness was her blessed state, an exultation. The stretching future thrilled her then like a book by an author she knew could be depended on. There was a book in the car, not so thrilling as that but good enough and better than going back into the crowd to find mummy and daddy and Cousin Arthur and Uncle George—much better! The car was parked on grass, in fact there was a notice saying 'The Paddock'. A flock of cars gently nibbling the grass. There was talk of getting a motor van to bring the milk at home—she hoped that wouldn't happen before they got back. The horse was called Jim and you could jump on the float for a lift when the nice milkman was driving. Home was another world. She desperately wanted the house and all its known corners. Like Hubert who was worried about the rabbits—who were probably being gorged on the green of the land. You could sit in the creaking inside of a car and with the doors open for air have a pleasant, leathery, reading silence of your own.

The cars returned the sun ringed in the myriad tiny scratches on their paint which nearly fried your hand to touch. But at the sight of their car's open doors she changed from hot and trailing. The doors had all been clumped shut by John she remembered quite distinctly. Two heads occu-

49

pied the back window. On all fours she reached the boot and settled cheek by jowl with the blowpipe. How out of breath she was! Seat-springs and creaks inside suggested the intense peculiarities of courting couples. The idea was enough for an explosion—Nigel and the goddess! Luckily, she was too short of breath. No, the goddess, preferring horses to cars, would gallop down on him, whisk him across the saddle, fling away his half-sucked ice-cream and implant a burning kiss on his cold mouth. Flicked through her mind a thought of Eleanour and Sir Rommel—rather shadowy for a day or so. *They* didn't need to kiss, in fact it was unthinkable: their contact was a thing of eyes and did not involve awful mouthy kissing.

It descended through the open door, resting the sandal they had all been treated to at breakfast on the parched grass. The whole thing was supported by a noose round Uncle George's big toe. This wiggled in a circular way and had a little copse of hairs on it. Seen that close, it had the horrible fascination of Nature Study worms. She studied it in Cousin Arthurish fashion to stave off giggling disaster. Familiar pipe-smoke floated down, soft bombs in the breathless air.

'That's it,' she heard him say, and filled in pipe-clenching, hairpin-gripping film mouths. Spies hang on against all odds. Doubts told her to creep off but this time it was more difficult. Something—the car mirror or a cracking joint—would give her away. Spies had specialised in the one consideration: not to be caught. 'We'd have been a bloody sight more private in Piccadilly Circus.'

'It's not my fault, is it?' Aunty Meg's voice that carried like her mother's, though they were only step-sisters. 'Freedom's a bit one-sided in these affairs.'

'Go on, blame me for coming. Considerable risk I might say. Why are we bashing our noodles on a brick wall? You tell me.'

'It's not for me to say, the way you put it.'

'There you go again. Make it my fault. Talk about the

spare proverbial. Bloody fiasco from start to finish.'

'This is the last day, George. I know we haven't had much chance to talk together.'

'Or the rest.'

'I know.'

The foot went up and out of sight. Janet grimaced. Unseen silences this time could not be sleep. She was almost relieved when she heard him brisk. 'I'm seeing this naval wallah for a few beers.'

'It's the last evening!'

'Up to you, Meg.'

'I've been about the documents.'

She raised her attention. This was more like.

'Maybe.' Uncle George.

'You know my position. You know my feelings.'

'I thought I did.'

'When will you be back?'

'This evening? Depends.'

'I'll be in the barn. So don't you come back loaded. You know, the big one.'

'When? Eleven?'

'Yes.'

'I'll take this then. Jack's not aiming to use it?'

'No. They talked about an early night.'

'Suits all round. I'll leave the car out of earshot and walk. I wasn't in Intelligence for nothing.'

'I know.' Pause. 'George?'

'Well?'

'I'll tell you all about the papers.'

'Could even do that. Hadn't we better pick up the pieces of your kids?'

'They're pretty tough, you know. Codliver oil and malt at school every day of the week.'

Smoothly Janet slipped into the shadow beneath the car from which she observed the two pairs of feet walking off. Without thinking of it, she waited for Uncle George to return and close the doors. She stayed on, studying the strange

51

underneath which smelt of oil and metal at rest. A touch of black greasiness marked her white shoulder. It would have to be explained when the time came. It was only a detail—not possibly the fatal false step.

FOUR

Pretending to sleep, Janet nearly had. Her mother's pilfered watch ticked its delicate time under the pillow, tickling the brink of silence. In the curtained bed Tricia was dormant. For the first time Tricia had not slept immediately, deciding instead to lecture her dolls—vast numbers of them—in a very bossy way. Now she snored. Janet got up to look at the time. It was only ten past ten. She wound the little wheel to encourage the passing night. An unhurried three-quarter moon gave light to see the time by. On the lino her feet touched each other, roots like a tree. She felt odd growing there in the moonlight and the moon when you looked at it became unfamiliar. Yet it was intimate with everybody and belonged separately to each.

She peeled off her long nightgown of light material and the soft broth of the moon swirled magic water up to her chest. With ages allotted to all the moves, she got into her knobbly pullover and the gymslippish dress, equally as dark. Sunburn would have to do to camouflage her face but she would dearly have liked black stockings. After all that it was not quite half past. Then she panicked. Of course they'd need to be there before eleven, as long before as possible. She had to get Cousin Arthur up. 'Millicent, be quiet!' She stopped, hunching her breath. Tricia scolding dolls in sleep.

Everything was moving, probably the watch too. A quick stuffing of the bed as in books produced an apologetic hump, but she had no time to improve it. Boards in the hall floor cried out and she walked almost into a brass bowl on a spindly table which had stationed itself outside the boys' room. Their door moved silently—something—and moonlight helped, tinkering with all the extraordinary objects in the room. Her father had christened it the Museum and John the youngest exhibit. Hubert, an even younger exhibit, was the first to be located, right on the edge of a bed big enough for six of him. She picked up his teddy but dared not move her brother. John was in his sleeping-bag on the floor: he'd practised at home. To get to Cousin Arthur she stepped over him.

William's face was upwards in moonlight; all he had over him was a sheet on top of which his arms lay quite straight. Altogether he was Sir Rommelish or like a statue she'd examined once in a church, a man of marble. Cutting these sliding images, she tapped on his chest as on a door. His eyes opening abruptly made her laugh.

'Shh. Time to get up.'

'I can't. I haven't got anything on.'

'That doesn't matter. I'll shut my eyes. Were you asleep?'

'Yes. That's why I didn't put my pyjamas on. It's so hot.'

'I've been awake all the time,' she said. 'We'll have to hurry.'

'Are your eyes shut?'

'Yes. Get a move on.'

He got up and hunted for clothes. She opened her eyes by accident.

'This what you're looking for?'

'Yes.' His teeth were making little noises.

'I thought you said you were hot.'

'I don't want to go.'

'Don't then.'

'Will you go?'

'Yes,' she said. 'I want to get to the bottom of the mystery.'

'It might be dangerous.'

'I know. I know a hiding place. I'm pretty good at hiding actually. If you like, I'll let you know what happens.'

'What's going to happen?'

'Well, I don't know that, do I? I suppose it'll be pretty elementary, my dear Watson.'

'I'm dressed now.'

54

'You don't *have* to come. If you do come you can be Arthur and I'm Eleanour. All right?'

'It's like ...' he hesitated for the right word, 'a conspiracy.'

'It's like a story,' she said. 'Which is why I thought of using our special names. There's heaps we could do if we had time. Putting a candle on the Bible.'

'Cutting our wrists for the blood to mingle.'

'Yes!' They both went *brrr* at the thought. Now the adventure was fun. Before it had been funny—moonlit and tomby; now it was more as it should be.

'Careful about treading on John.' They got through the door which creaked this time. She warned about the floorboards. 'It's like walking on mice.'

The stairs turned a corner half way down. She stopped him with her hand. Below, a door was opening. 'Are you sure you had it at the fête?'

'Pater,' she whispered. 'Mum's watch. I've got it.' The door closed. She remembered other evenings and the strange, overheard evening lives of parents. A ticking, not the watch, stopped her. Not the grandfather clock which had stopped, Mr Chauvel said, the minute the Germans landed on island soil. Cousin Arthur's teeth. 'Really,' she hissed. 'This isn't even the dangerous part.' But was relieved all the same to be out in the dark and round one or two corners.

'Will that man from the torpedo boat be there?'

'What?' A soft *shush* which had fumbled at her heart turned itself into a cow on the far side of the wall. 'I don't know. I think so. They said documents.'

'It might be a map of the gold the Nazis left.' For the first time he sounded eager. And the eagerness of his face, a white pennant—like the cow's breathing, seemed to startle her.

'It could be.'

'Or something else.' That reassured her. Not as definite as a cow—and few things are, his voice suggested he had jumped to other ideas and to explanations which would stand daylight.

For now it was the easier business of getting into the barn. She knew of a sort of manger at one end, a perfect perch. There

55

was even a separate entrance via steps at the back. 'Careful,' she whispered at the foot of them.

'It's only the fifth one that's wonky.'

'How do you know?' She was almost annoyed.

'I counted them,' he said.

'I suppose this was one of the places you went looking for bats.'

'I've been here.'

Still she was leading the way, treading with a general caution and trying not to count the treads, but she took a big step over the fifth. In the sunlight the door was of grey, exhausted wood; the moon plated everything with its own colour. It looked immovable and did not give. He came up beside her, thumbed the latch and pushed it open.

'Sort of lift it,' he said.

'I'm glad you came.' If that was sarcasm it was fairly unintentional. Through the doorway the darkness had a finer weave. 'Inside of a cow's tummy at midnight.' Her father, the comfort of using his words.

Arthur wanted to know the time and she put her wrist outside. 'Ten to.'

She was pleased to be the one who remembered to close the door. 'We mustn't sneeze either.' Straw was thick in the air and doing things to your nose.

'You there?'

'Ow.'

'Mind out!'

Janet moved his knee from her chest. It felt quite bony. 'Sorry.'

'We mustn't fall over the edge.'

'Not likely.'

'This is really a balcony,' he said. 'I'll crawl and find out when it stops.'

'Find out *before* it stops. I said we'd have a grandstand view.'

'Here.'

She wriggled along to him. The cavern of the main barn

developed slowly in front of their eyes. Cousin Arthur said he had some sweets.

'We ought to eat carrots. You know, to see in the dark. On second thoughts they might be a bit noisy.'

He said, 'Carrot drops.'

'Ugh. I used to think cough-drops were to make you cough.'

A rustle to feel for. 'They're a bit stuck up.'

'Snob-drops.' She pulled one off. 'Arthur,' she said when it was sucked smooth, 'you know the War? We had prisoners and some children caught one in a barn like this. They waited and waited and the police came. He was only an Italian but they got "commended" by the Girl Guides or somebody. Mary Black was one—she *used to be* my best friend. It was in the papers. She said he cried.'

'My father interviewed them. You know, to get information. It was mostly German sailors. He said they were jolly pleased to be captured and pretty harmless really.'

'You can't be afraid of enemies if they cry. I don't think they're coming. I think your Uncle George took the papers and went on the U boat.'

'It was an MTB. U boats are submarines and they don't have them now. They were all captured.'

'Perhaps some weren't. They could easily hide in under-water caves and have steps cut out of the rock so they could put on ordinary clothes and go shopping. Then they'd go off at night in the submarine.'

'And he's not a real uncle.'

'So you've said.' Another sweet, another time to be silent. Janet sucked on a new idea, one that had been there all along in a corner. Cousin Arthur's father had been in the Navy and could still be. Aunty Meg had definitely mentioned documents. Mr Straker had talked with the motor-boat man, also navy. The sweet, perfectly rounded by the tip of her tongue, moved with these thoughts thoughtfully along the counting-house of her teeth. Hadn't 'Uncle George' wanted to get William on the boat? The poor uncle, her own real uncle whom she'd never met, could easily be somehow being kept

57

like a prisoner away from Aunty Meg. An explosion; she had bitten through the sweet—which she always did and always meant not to. The cave with steps of course was too much like a story.

But when the big door rattled violently it wasn't. Someone scraped enough room to get in. Their noisiness was incredible until she realised they would not expect listeners. Even before the white jacket showed, it was obvious. All noises announced him. His breathing filled the place; he sneezed like a thunderclap.

They lay on ice. No chance of them sneezing. They breathed the tiniest nosefuls and grew small.

His torch shot like a rocket to the ceiling, then scribbled round the walls.

'Bloody hell.

'Serve you bloody right,' said Uncle George. 'Jesus!'

They could see without raising their heads because the balcony had holes in it; it was a sort of lattice with hay on. For spying it was safe—safer than the wall of the fort, much safer than the boot of the car. Now Uncle George was dancing with a bucket on his foot, clanking and swearing. The torch danced its own dance, blinking right into their eyes or scuttling in the rafters. She had suddenly relaxed, like swimming or riding a horse. William's hand when she found it was tightly clenched and did not loosen with coaxing. She welled over for him—he was so thin and so tied up. Her superiority wasn't the sort to pride itself, for it scooped everything tenderly.

'He's put his foot in it,' she whispered. Her fingers stroked his which stayed in a knot. 'What next?'

Next the bucket came off. The torch swung round and settled on it. There was a lot of breathing. Then he took a running kick at the bucket which promptly flew into a high corner and stuck there. The light spotted it and he sighed.

They were still looking, and he was, when Aunt Meg slipped in. Women make less disturbance moving about. She was there beneath them.

58

'Bit bloody late, aren't you?'

'If you're going to be awkward ...'

'I don't like being nagged.'

'Who is?'

'Every bloody thing. Sorry, Meg. You know what I'm like. Want a list?'

'All right.'

'Inland Revenue. Bloody Gladys—*and* her relations. Kids. *Anno Domini.*'

'Not Margaret Goodyear?'

'I'm not worthy of you. I'm not worthy to lick your boots.'

'You can do better than that.' She laughed. 'That sounds like the beer talking.'

'It's not. I'm forty next month. What have I got to show for it?'

'As much as anyone else.'

'What's that? Failing eyesight, Meg. Failing everything else. All storeys including the basement.'

'I'm sorry—you make me laugh when you feel sorry for yourself. I've told you I've no complaints.'

'You're a forgiving girl. You are, Meg. You've got a heart of gold. A twenty-two bloody carat heart. Meg?'

They were almost underneath in foreshortened view between the slats and lit by the spillage of torchbeam shining among their feet. Nothing Janet could do, no way out, no telling now what next. Those documents and U boats had never existed, not even in her mind.

'You were right about those jars. I'll need helping. You know, help.'

William's hands had moved; now they were in his eye-sockets. Where his fingers sometimes touched for better sight, his fingers knotted hard as cricket-balls pressed against his lids, creating inside another world where shapes and lights were made from the inside—the work of his secret blood. Replacing the other world.

*   *   *

'Those burlesque dancers haven't got half of what you've got.'
'You want?'
'You don't even need corsets, Meg.'

What were they doing? He was holding the light and Aunty Meg was doing something behind her own back. The light held until something came off and shadows swam into the beam. Great eyes which were the nipples. Then out went the torch, or actually into the straw, making a bright little nest for itself. In the new darkness they lumped together and the sounds of the fort—only clear, very clear—filled the barn. And she knew. And she knew she had known all along.

They were on a common, of accord all tired of the sea—though it was there, other islands studding it and France a mysterious smear on the horizon. The sun was the same; the perfection of the weather tiresome. To her everything was. The picnic was a madness of packets and jars and lost cups. All this trouble to eat! And the whole point of having it here to avoid sand, with the grass full of sand and of insects as well. On a beach at least she could have run across pebbles, across sharp rocks and plunged in. She knew however that the sea was no good. She was pinned into the day and nothing in the world could offer relief.

Her father was at his worst. He had the baby under one arm and Hubert and two toddlers collected from somewhere and he was mending Tricia's boat and helping John put up the striped awning thing. He was also imitating a llama. She loved him; she could cry out. The sandwich was of use that Aunt Meg passed over for, biting it, she nearly bit out her tongue. Pain was a small relief.

'Roll up! Janny, got your ticket? Show's starting in two minutes. Hubert, ticket here.'

He didn't know. None of them did, not even Aunty Meg. To themselves they were all the same. To her, lead weights stuck as she drowned.

'Sit in rows.' Hubert pulling her hand.

60

'Why on earth?' Games with children were especially unbearable.

'Ladies and gentlemen ...' Her father.

Janet scraped the sandy soil with her heel. Tricia, she noticed, had walked off. In the green-white light of the awning Hubert and the other little two were trying to think of a performance. It was the one thing they had not thought about. Hubert attempted a somersault and the others did some hopping. They had a confab. It was so clear—their surprise and embarrassment. It bubbled up to her through her suffocation. Her mother's 'Bravo!' and clapping seemed to miss by miles what registered itself with a sad weariness as a pricking at the back of her eyes.

'Who's going to round up the boys?'

'I will.' She leapt up.

'Good girl. I hope they haven't broken their necks in the castle. We'd have heard a land-mine.'

She raced up paths through scratchy bracken. There was no Sir Rommel flying at her elbow and the castle was a certain area enclosed with walls of stone. By endowing nothing she might survive. She had to exist but could leave the world for what it was—stones, bracken, the swimming blueness. John gunned her down from the ramparts.

'Da-da-*dah*!'

To humour him she raised her hands. 'The picnic's ready. Seen William?'

'There's a Russian naval gun. You ought to see it. They've taken most of them away. It's a German one.'

'That hardly answers my question.' Here she was already being the big sister. 'Thought you said Russian?'

'They captured it, silly. What would Russians be doing here?'

'The food's ready. I've told you anyway.'

A long stumbly path took her round and through a gateway. The interior of the castle would have been disappointing if she had been looking for anything from it. Cousin Arthur —plain William Goodyear—was sitting on a tower. She

61

joined his inspection of the tiny harbour away down at their feet.

'It seems the sandwiches are ready.' She could as easily have said anything. Since the barn they had not spoken.

'Did Aunty Liz get her watch back?'

'Yes.' His question did not surprise her. 'I left it in her beach shoe. In the end she remembered leaving it there! You know how it is—they talked about nothing else at breakfast. You had yours earlier, didn't you?'

'To go down to the boat you mean?'

'I didn't exactly. Mr Straker got off all right, I suppose.'

'He gave us these. My mother said not to. This is yours.'

'But it's a pound!' She held it as if it threatened to blow away, which it did in the lightest of breezes. 'He didn't give one to John I hope.'

'One to me and one to my sister. One each for you and John and Hubert and the baby. He forgot Mark I think.'

'That's six pounds!'

'I'll give the others to Uncle Anstey.'

'It might be as well.'

She felt the holiday was over already and they were saying goodbye on some platform. As if Cousin Arthur was in a grey suit and whisking off into his life again. Yet there were days and days to go. They yawned again. That was what the sinister Uncle George had done: come out of nowhere and left nothing behind but money, staggering amounts you didn't want and yet couldn't help feeling respectful about. A whole pound, six whole pounds! But he had left a gaping hole, like the quarries they had round here. Sir Rommel had gone for one, not that he mattered all that much. Now it was impossible to hope for anything from poor, stiff William. At the end of the holiday—she glimpsed it, it all—she might have found a far different cousin than Uncle George had left her. A hole, a terrible hole. They couldn't speak of it, they couldn't speak of anything. All they could do was to play the parts of children until the real platforms. It was a great, shifting puzzle and nothing was certain. They walked down the steps and out of the castle.

'I'll hand the money over when we get there,' he said. It was not his real self talking.

In the springtide of her temporary understanding one rock stood: her blame. Uncle George had had all these terrible effects but what of her: was she guilty, as in hymns? Was that, finally, possible?

While the tide was running back, whilst they were walking down, Janet searched herself for guilt. It was too well hidden. Her body moved, full of nothing but itself and marvellous and quite blameless. The great blue sea absolved her as well. She turned to William, who was coming more carefully behind her, with a laugh bubbling up from nowhere. 'Aren't picnics *awful?*'

BOOK TWO

BOOK TWO

ONE

'Not a bad night. Do you want a 'go with my matches?' The older man thumbed down burning St Bruno. 'These ancient courts,' he said suddenly.

William looked into his own pipe, which had never amounted to a success. 'Burnt out.'

'These courts you mean?' Dr Earwaker bubbled contentedly. 'Nip of autumn certainly. Yes, they're so bloody old, aren't they? Those who built these, what would they think of us scientists? Burn us in the Market Square soon as look at us.'

'Venerable.'

'They make me feel my age somehow. I can't work that one out. Or it's the fen air. You smelt the night-scented stock through there? You ought to.'

'I lived there in my third year.'

'Gave you sweet dreams then.'

They lingered on outside Hall, footworn flags beneath their feet—the bed of time's slowest river. They were both half reluctant to get off. William found Dr Earwaker as agreeable on dining nights as anyone else. S.C.R., they said, was likely to be tough going in the coming term.

'This won't do. I lead the usual double life. Tonight it's moving paving stones. Mavis has one of her bursts on. They usually end in low back-strain. I'll imagine you sitting with your windows open.'

'Goodnight.' William watched him as far as the Porters' Lodge where the Head Porter—a good deal more like a film don than most dons were—touched his bowler.

He wondered if Earwaker was merely being kind to him,

if that was it. No. In a hovering sort of way they had made contact. Some places could be over-civilised as others savage; in either case real contact became difficult, precarious certainly. But what was real contact? Were friendships in the general run, bumpings-into, was the whole normal distribution of acquaintance *unreal*? He walked slowly round the cloisters. They oppressed him very much tonight. Yet they were the best in Cambridge: the least civic, the most homely. Somehow, as Earwaker had hinted, these buildings were too old to attach to; like rocks favoured by seabirds, too encrusted with attachment. Rarely thinking in comparisons, he found this one self-defeating. Birds of a feather did flock to one site. Unlike that of nearly everyone else on High Table, his training did not puff the individual.

William came to the paving stone which was carved deeply with a seventeenth century name and date. They did things properly in those days; unless it was a gravestone, the whim of an atheistical Fellow, an ancient academic joke? And at the tunnel there which led into Maple Tree Court he was arrested by the scent of gillyflowers. He went through, remembering his old room and remembering too—with the odd clarity of things unremembered since—something in his childhood to do with deliberate sniffing and listening. It had been a small mistake on Earwaker's part to think of him here still. Only two years ago he had been totally familiar with this part of college. Now it was digs. It was his fifth year around the place; there were plenty for whom it was fifty. Five or fifty. Gillyflowers. He sniffed.

Suddenly the scent sketched in the immensity of his desolation. He needed no reminding but stopped, caught, sniffing like one of the animals academically concerning him. Desolation spread as if seen for the first time, more infinite than space. Even his heartbeat was affected, he noted. William studied his pipe like some puzzling, alien object. The white lettering at the foot of the staircase said—'2. Rattenbury, R.' Two layers down it was 'Goodyear, W. A.' Some whistling man came each summer and painted you out, and that was that.

68

His digs were walkable, if you liked walking. The percentage of each day spent walking was significant. The digs were scented with nothing, except—perhaps—coalgas; loneliness perhaps. Mrs Sugden was still full of 'the gentleman a year or so back' who had done himself in. Eight years in fact, as William had discovered elsewhere. She had the canary which was the twist in the tale. The gentleman had placed a cushion in the oven and the canary he had moved out into the hall.

Although used to different rooms, his life an annual succession of them since his mother's divorce had whisked him suddenly to a minor public school in the north; and although publicly claiming an indifference to surroundings (to suggest inner riches?)—William had in three weeks flat developed a relationship with the Sugden digs. Entering the hall for example produced a specific feeling of homelessness. The canary, original or replacement, scuttled briefly. Whichever it was, it no longer lived at risk in the kitchen. Inevitably Mrs Sugden would then open the lounge door, her inevitable 'Oh, it's you,' somehow intoned to deny the fact.

The room itself was overpowering. The room itself was completely green. Nothing would brighten it. The light at which, as often as he was there, he stared, was a thing of iron and frosted glass—a square umbrella generating infra-red light, holding the room in thrall. In it William saw himself as living out an anti-life on the model of anti-matter once mentioned by Earwaker—Earwaker being a physicist at the frontiers when not breaking primary laws and getting low back-strain.

The streets were deserted more or less, high summer lulling between tourists and students, Night and the mist which popularly emanated from 'the fens' aquatinting the colleges. He stopped at Jarry's for half a pint. The barman was on his favourite topic: 'Best Pimm's in town. Mind you, I need notice—a day for preference but an hour for necessity. Next time you're having any young lady up, sir, give it a thought.'

He said he would. The man was being friendly, or business-like. But if all the young ladies he knew were to drink Pimm's twenty-four hours a day Jarry's would go down the sink. A huge log fire burned: Jarry's was run on professional rather than commercial principles. The only other customer, a rather beautiful girl reading the re-christened *Guardian*, seemed to be drinking lemonade and any great rush later on was unlikely. In the life he might have led he thought of her reading his eyes instead ... casual thought.

He settled on a settle. Outwardly, to the barman for instance, he must be what he almost was—the trim young don in flannels and good tweed jacket, complete with pipe. The fire danced in his beer.

Returning to the desolation of Maple Tree Court, he did so with scientific deliberation. Jarry's fire was superb, a pseudo-organism using oxygen to release energy at a spanking rate. As the girl might, jiving at the jazz club over the bicycle shop. Or himself and Earwaker in the Market Square. 'Mavis was never like this,' as Earwaker's lumbar region ceased to give trouble; himself replying, 'Venerable,' and his pipe for the first and last time properly lit. And he heard old Corbett—one of very few saving graces of the school in the north—claiming again that 'all mortal things' would sustain rational examination. How the old boy had believed it—transmitting the Light! And a few of them carried old Corbett's faith with them as the bodies of saints there in the dripping north (Cuthbert and Aidan, Bede? Earwaker?) had been endlessly moved on by increasingly befogged believers.

His own desolation was immeasurable, a check; otherwise it bore rational examination only too readily. Its infinity seemed exact, not exaggeration. William's strength to face it, which he knew he had, was again—not negative—but the inverse of the usual palliative. He saw without condescension that love and business (all activities save Corbett's prescription) corresponded to huddlings in the cave against primeval night. No false heroics were required to sustain his stance of gaper-out. The needs were all known to him, shape by shape; he could survive without filling in those shapes. With work

70

his intellectual position might become truly ascetic. Those sneezing saints had managed it.

Metaphysics was their business, biology his. Where they crossed played hell with saints. Lucky then to have sat at Corbett's feet instead of Bede's. He had too—the dear old boy perched up on the master's bench 'I want every interested boy to see and understand this ...' Ecologically, the taking of a mate was less universal than was universally believed. As many human matings were culturally as biologically determined. Cultural pressures in his case had been slight. The minor public school had been more or less directly followed by these mostly male groves. There had been one or two agonies and one or two inconclusive episodes. Now he was a normal adult male but celibate. Bad luck but good ecology. Corbett had preached the sifting of all evidence and that meant reference to psychology. Most psychologists he knew spent their time tinkering with pigeons' brains like latter-day augurists. He had read all the Penguins however and knew who Freud was.

Which got him to the bottom of his glass if nothing else. The stroll to Sugdens' was almost inviting. Getting up, he noticed that the departure of his *Guardian* angel had taken place as he sat rapt.

Money rattled lightly in the tin. The man he had taken over from had called him 'Comrade'. Hiding in a shop doorway, he felt foolish and righteous, more foolish than righteous. Fortunately it was half-day closing and the public was not much in evidence. At the end of an hour someone would relieve him. An hour dangling a tin was nothing: his trepidation measured how draught-proof he had made his life. Sugdens', College, the lab, the field experiment. Still, he had taken it on. On the same scale that meant something.

Gore, jerking up from the microscope and surfacing from his wild hair, had said: 'Do you support the coloured South Africans in principle, Goodyear?'

He had said so.

71

He dropped in half-a-crown, not forgetting Wood who fed his experimental mosquitoes on his own blood. The tin was made for the job with a round hole to breathe in notes and a slit to gulp coins. Round it in red S. AFRICAN DEFENCE FUND. Gore in his terrible, abrupt way had mentioned pamphlets but the previous dangler had passed on only the tin. As donors might reasonably want to know what they were supporting, William had tried to ask for information but the man had only said out of the corner of his beard: 'Watch out for proctors and coppers, comrade. We're doing this without bene-fit of clergy.' Then he had looked at him and at his sports coat, as if wanting to take the tin back or, more likely, the word 'comrade' before making a bee-line across the road.

The tin did not sustain much rational examination. Hearing footsteps, he advanced it. A cleric accelerated by, too old a bird to catch with chaff. Two pennies came out of his own pocket—1918 and 1939. Britannia had adjusted her draperies between the wars and picked up a lighthouse. He fed them in one at a time. The hour ahead yawned uniquely. If only he had brought the proofs of the *Trichoniscus* paper. He hoarded the wealth of flanking shopwindows. There were displays to savour and pricetags to read. Prisoners in solitary killed more time with less. He'd had an impression of drapery; turning to conspire with his reflection, he saw two shopgirls kneeling by a dummy. Their lips were glued together but wild giggles got out at their eyes. One of them as he stared got up and with a small flourish lowered green dress material to reveal plaster breasts. They were large but without nipples. He stared on and the girls turned their heads away, exploding and spitting pins. William lowered his eyes. 'A bargain @ 8/11 the yard.'

No way suggested itself of raising his eyes. Abject defeat. Pedantically, he noted the archaism of '8/11 the yard.' His head hung in its shame and abject defeat. There was no amelioration.

Then the door was unbolted and a girl came out, the one who had not bared the plaster breasts. 'We couldn't help watching,' she said. 'And you *was* funny putting in your own money. You can't deny it. Here.' She took the tin and dropped in sixpence. 'Rattle it around a bit.'

'Thanks.' He could think of nothing else to say. Shopgirls—traditionally from Woolworth's, were legendary in Cambridge—in every sense. There had been Crathorne daring convention in a black leather jacket—a specialist, according to him. Shopgirls were featured performing all sorts of kind acts, but never like this.

'You don't have to mind Jean.'

'No, I don't.' It was true. So when he had customers—the woman don who posted a rolled note, saying 'Damn right, too'; the old body who told him she'd never stand for being blind ('I'd grope me way to the gas-stove')—he acknowledged their dumbshow applause with discreet bows. The hour ended quickly, a clear case of doing yourself good by doing good unto others. When the girls trooped off he was sorry. Calling 'Ta-ta' they legged it between the first drops of a rain which steadily put on weight so that his relief appeared masked in a sodden gown.

'They told me you had a beard. One lot did. Another lot told me you were from Girton. I'm new. Does it often do this?'

'Now and then.' The newcomer had the bright interest of new arrivals in his face. William felt an old lag. It had taken him five years to turn out for an unselfish principle and this one had managed it in five days. Though the passing stream of undergraduates was so large—dons and researchers responding at best with humane tolerance—something: the freshman's face or the rain or even the legacy of the shopgirls —made William hang on, picturing the possibilities lying before this particular eighteen-year-old.

'First year, are you?'

'We matriculated this morning. That's why I'm in this suit. It was a bit of a farce, walking to the ... Senate House. This guy spouting Latin. I'm doing English, sorry, *reading* it. So far we've all been buying cheap kettles. It happens every year, of course. Sorry.'

'It did in 'fifty-five.'

'Blimey you must be a Senior Member ... Staff.'

'Research,' said William.

The freshman shook his head. 'What in?'

'Ecology, basically.'

'I don't even know what that is.'

'Well, instead of looking at things individually—animals and plants—you take the life-support systems into account. You are so many cows, so many acres of wheat and the rest of it in your lifetime.'

'I'd never thought of that. Do you give lectures?'

'No. And they wouldn't be worth listening to. I do do practicals. I'm doing one now, almost.'

'You'll get soaked.'

'The marvels of modern science.' William pulled out his plastic mac which folded up in your pocket if your pocket was capacious enough and disintegrated on excitable wearers. He had had it two years.

'Let me give you my address.' The freshman pencilled on something from his wallet. 'You might be that way sometime, caught without your mac. I'll be bogged down in Middle English. Ecology would cheer me up.'

William stowed away the paper and set off. Two hours teaching the counting of *Daphnia* and use of microscopes. The last hour had been itself a sort of practical. A topic of conversation with the abrupt and mesmeric Gore—something as well against a rainy day.

He had been at it since morning. Sunday was still the best day to get a good spell in, though not as good as a year ago, which had not been as good as a year before that. Everyone was becoming more efficient and harder working—or taking longer to do less. The new decade with exponentially increasing PhDs seemed to be demanding more application and less speculation. The demonstrations of his own first year had been more exciting, uncertain and unsound than the present variety. Results had been cooked more openly in the decade before that

74

and in the prehistory of before the War ... some anecdotes still lingered in the modernised labs but they were dying the death. William's thoughts had wandered this way partly through finding a whole group of second-years wordlessly at work in the constant-temperature room and partly through having spent the whole dull November day around the funnel-room, extracting the fauna of a woodland floor (randomly sampled) and counting them. His right eye was beginning to seize up. It watered—scientist's eye, like housemaid's knee but less interesting.

Gore that morning had expressed surprise that instant-coffee manufacturers did not freeze-dry their product. Coming from him, that was conversation.

Bill looked at his results, figures not yet results. The day's work was a fraction of the whole. 'Rome wasn't built in a day,' Smithers had announced last week. By that token all these figures added up to one brick. Who could extrapolate houses from a brick? A fragment of one of his forays into Culture came to him: 'He found Rome brick and left it marble.' Smithers of course was hoping to find his thesis brick and marble-face it in the definitive work rumour said he was at.

The lights on the funnel-bank clicked off by courtesy of the time-switch. Heat drove the little beggars further and further down into their transported environment until they dropped with a micro-ping into an awaiting tray. One man had spent years on locusts. William recalled their little sub-human faces as they climbed over one another in the heated enclosure. He had asked the man if ever he felt like Hitler. 'They like it,' he'd said. 'Really it's no worse than the Underground, is it? It's better—like the Ritz really.'

Occasionally Bill doubted what he was doing, doubted Corbett, doubted the lot. Especially now when scientist's eye blinked to give him two sets of figures, wobbly window-frames, a time-switch nightfall and a Universe like a laboratory, God saying: 'Really, it's no worse than Hell, is it?'

He reviewed possibilities—dinner in Hall with discussion

75

afterwards over coffee and perhaps brandy. The most interesting senior members all seemed to live at a distance, beetling off as soon as they could. Everyone said it was different at Oxford; there, everyone said, you entertained cabinet ministers and sparkled over your port. Here you rushed off to wife and kids, or to move paving stones. None of the people he could think of did he feel like, though he liked a good number of them. He remembered the Defence Fund of five weeks before; the address was still in his wallet near the labs. The name looked more like St Austel than anything, conjuring up cardboard earls of nineteenth-century romance: some good wireless adaptations.

On the way out he ran into Gore and said goodnight. Gore seemed to say 'half a jiff' but it might have been his catarrh. William was crossing the large area of concrete where surveyors' poles staked out the glorious future when Gore swept up on his bike and landed, dancing in puddles. 'Don't you have a bicycle?'

He was almost too surprised to speak and when he did it had to be the whole story—how he had been knocked off his machine by the opening of a limousine's door, how the culprits having picked him up had said 'God, we need a drink' and disappeared into the nearest hotel. He had needed three stitches himself and a new front wheel which he had never bothered to get.

Gore shook his hair. 'Were your forks all right? A wheel's nothing. Forks can be hell.'

'Probably.' William felt like asking outright what Gore wanted. A Gore-ish question, but then did people like Gore depend on the social norms in others? Would it offend or would it unlock what had remained sealed for a good two years? Having got that far, William was prompted to the rest by scientific training. 'What do you want, Gore?'

'A chat.'

They stopped, with Gore looking around perhaps to make sure enough concrete was isolating them. November dripped miserably.

76

'The point is, Goodyear, marriage. I'm twenty-four. If I start now it might be two years before I marry. That makes me twenty-six. If we're both normally fertile it means offspring by the time I'm thirty—bit earlier perhaps. The current human generation is down to about twenty-five, isn't it? I can't see how it can all be done in a year but I'd better start now.'

William smiled uncertainly in dazed encouragement; Gore may even have made a joke. 'Are you asking me as an ecologist?'

'No. Christ, no! I'm a physiologist. No disrespect to your Charlie Eltons and Odums; but, Christ, no. Frankly, Goodyear, I've not much idea how to set about it.'

'You want me to be a sort of marriage bureau? Produce a sample for you?'

Gore considered it hopefully, then shook his head. 'Don't think that's on, Goodyear. You bloody ecologists.' He laughed heartily.

'You're a physiologist, come to that.'

'Insects. I don't want to marry an insect.' They both laughed. It was unheard of. 'You know,' said Gore. 'Where to find them.'

'Girls?'

'That sort of thing, yes.'

'I don't know if I do. There's the jazz club, but the competition's stiff. How about Christian groups? I went to an SCM meeting once.'

'I don't want any child of mine befuddled with mystic twaddle. Would you ... come with me, Goodyear, if it comes to that?'

'All right.'

Gore swung into the saddle and cycled away, his tyres sprouting rainbows.

William remained. He felt pleased with himself for being charitable and at the same time pleased that Gore should have singled him out as an expert in the field.

The road St Austel lodged in was reposing in the incipient

nightfall—a Victorian terrace of plain-faced houses. He liked their simplicity. The Sugdens' house was a specimen from the other end of the era; between these and that burgeoning wealth had added pinnacles and carvings which by 1910 had left only traces, vestigeal motifs. The simplicity of 1910 was impoverished; Sugdens' would have looked *passé* from the start. Stanwick Street was exactly right for St Austel to live in. William's recollection of him clarified—it was mainly of an open quality, something he may not have noticed at the time, something he'd grown unconsciously aware of since. The irrationality of this was self-evident—a meeting of moments, no contact since, a few maundering thoughts about house-architecture and then, coming up to 35 Stanwick Street, quite a keen expectation.

Opposite there was an orchard and the bare sticks of an apple-tree over its high stone wall took part in his new, indefinite perceptions. He surmised reaction to long hours in the funnel-room or a by-product of the exchange with Gore. Somewhere in the region of reflex lay the explanation—an arm pressed against a wall rising of its own volition. Yet, irrationally, whatever it was persisted. He rang, confident.

There was nothing about the orchard wall to mark it out, nothing about the tree.

The door opened at his back. A girl there. He asked if it was the house.

'St Austel? I don't think so. Is that his name?'

'Half a minute.' William fumbled in his wallet. 'Here.'

She looked and laughed in the swing of her hair. 'It's Hubert. What's he been up to? Anstey.'

'Wait a minute. You're Janet.'

'Yes.'

'I'm William, er, Goodyear.'

'Arthur. Good heavens.'

'Isn't it? I didn't expect to meet you when I woke up this morning.'

'That's one way of looking at it. Do you expect to expect things? Second sight? Cup of tea?'

78

'Please. He said something about cheap kettles.'

'Cheap, my foot. All-electric.'

Hubert's rooms were *rooms* rather than digs. There were two, inter-joining, small but almost elegant. The view was that of the winter orchard. They were furnished with taste. There was a lot to talk about, starting with the rooms. He learned directly that Hubert was fortunate in his Welsh landlady, indirectly that Janet was specially fond of him. Trying hard, he could not remember Hubert as a child, nor Janet much.

'Do you take sugar? I can't be expected to remember after all this time.'

'I didn't expect you to. One and a half, please.' William's word-play had not exactly worked but he felt at ease with her and altogether outside his normal mode. She sat on her legs in the corner of a neo-Graecian settee not unlike the one in the SCR priced by Earwaker at fifty pounds. The dress she had on was of very dark tartan topped with a demure white collar but the skirt was short and studying the settee he had studied her knees. She was as neat as a cat.

'Isn't it strange? Would you have recognised me? Do you remember that holiday a few years after the War?'

'No to the first part and yes to the second. Your hair's darker,' he said.

'What are you doing here?'

'Research.'

They had got through the relations—his sister running a dress-shop in London; her brother John flying with the Royal Air Force—by the time Hubert got back with parcels and people.

'Hullo! Nice to see you. I looked up "ecology", tried it in an essay, with dire results. Probably used it wrongly. You've met Janet. My big sister.'

'And he's your big cousin, half-cousin or whatever we are.'

'William. So he is!' Dumping foodstuffs, Hubert looked at him with complete attention.

'Hubert's got this fantastic memory, if that's what it is. Haven't you, dear?'

'If you say so. Tom, Dick and Harry—friends.'

'I know,' she said. 'I couldn't believe it at first. I'll brew fresh tea but you can do the rest. When in Cambridge I expect to be punted or crumpeted, depending on the season.'

'I have sisters,' said Tom, or Dick, or Harry when she had gone out with teapot; it was said by way of explanation.

'Here we all are,' said Hubert, 'having tea in my rooms!'

'You can never believe the things that are.' Dick or Harry or Tom spoke affectionately.

'He enjoys them. Don't you, old cock?' Harry, Tom or Dick pronged a crumpet.

To William they were all bright sparks, indistinguishable. He happily nursed the sense of being an outsider; age came into it—of an age with Janet.

'Are you all doing Eng Lit?'

'That's right. All being educated above our station and fitted for private incomes we'll never have. The best that was thought and written—by private incomes. I think of the Moscow Metro, a royal palace for the People. I'm Tom Thorpe.'

'Who's been to Mos-cow. He had to get that in. I'm Richard Manghan, only "Dick" when with these two trollops.'

'Trollops?' said Hubert. 'That's a new one. Which leaves Harry. Harold in fact—Harold Orton.'

'Sounds familiar.' They laughed politely. For the life of him William could not pin down the august personage he'd referred to.

Hubert explained that Thorpe had been at school with him. 'Richard and Harold are new.'

'New is not what I feel. I did my bloody time in Cyprus.' Manghan opened the door.

'I don't want to join the army' faded out at 'hang around' in the face of Janet. She said: 'Don't mind me—I know it.'

'Two years of my life.' Manghan was nearly as tall as the door, dark-featured, touched with bitterness.

'If you're going to talk about the guns you've fired, or haven't fired, I'm going.' Janet dealt cups, saucers and plates

80

like cards. 'One brother flying jets round Canada is quite sufficient.'

'He likes it.' Hubert's crumpet went up in smoke. 'It appeals to the poetry in him.'

'John never had any in him.'

Hubert got rid of the remains. 'We all have.'

'Ha!' Harold bellowed.

'It's true.'

The unusual thing about Hubert, it now seemed to William, was an absence of defensiveness—he said what he meant without bluntness.

'I grant you Manghan. Scholars cite documents. I'm a mere Exhibitioner but I cite documents.' Orton fingered through his briefcase. 'Next week's *Granta*. An advance copy of what the world is waiting for.'

Manghan was still in the doorway. 'Must you?'

'I must. Not only poetry, but also a sonnet. No, if you publish you have to be damned. Like the *Daily Mirror*.'

'With faint praise,' said Tom. 'Look, can't we have our tea in peace?'

'Respectful 'ush in the presence of Art. This is literally literary: a work of literature with literary overtones.'

'Stuff it.'

'The poet speaks. Is ...'

'William,' said William.

'Are you a connoisseur of sonnets?'

'Scientist.'

'Bill's an ecologist.' Hubert made a great deal of the word—defending him? Orton was not to be stopped.

' "To the Only Begetter of the Ensuing Sonnet: Mr W. S." Isn't that witty?'

'For Christ's sake, Orton.' Thorpe sounded bored. Manghan had not moved. William balanced his cup uncertainly. Orton read:

' "Why should I shower praise on beauty and
Then instruct one to perpetuate it,

Extol the product of my mind and hand
When Time will show—alas—I over-rate it?
All you poets made your bragging good
And now your musty sonnets are raked through
By us whose Age is made of softer wood:
For all our skill it's obvious we fake you.
In fact I fancy Verse has had its day
And we are serious only in despair,
Slipping the passions you made pay
Like jokers in the pack. And yet we care.
And yet we are as fitted as you, Bards,
Whose lives were played like instruments, not cards."
Fitted for what?' Orton asked, making scarcely a pause be-
tween his question and Manghan's punchline.

'To live.' Hubert was quick in another way. 'That's what
Dick means. I like it.'

'I don't follow the wood image,' said Orton.

'For pity's sake. Do you all analyse everything all the
time? At least Bill keeps that for his lab, don't you?'

'Results, I suppose.'

'There you are then,' Janet said.

'Merely I was saying ...' said Orton but said no more.

'The critic!' Tom Thorpe waved arms. ' "Merely I was saying"—did you hear him? If you're going to be mere, don't
bother. I'm trivial or profound but never sodding *mere*. The
poem's O.K. Let's drink to it.'

Janet stepped neatly over abandoned male legs to pour the
tea.

The talk ranged, but never far from Literature. William,
whose reading had been directed by chance, was impressed.
Literature always gave something to talk about, something to
pop into at the drop of a name. It gave body to conversation.
Janet was at home in it without initiating many changes of
direction; Orton and Manghan were clearly the leaders and
their annoyance with each other gave edge. Thorpe was
easier, sniffing for jokes, being funny. Hubert's presence was
distinct but outside categories. It was as if William had never

82

been to a Cambridge tea before—that labour in vain with toasting forks, the balance of ideas and teacups. He had probably notched up one a week for five years. A foraging party brought back beer and chips; tea shaded imperceptibly into supper.

'When's your train, sis?'

'Half nine.'

'If we start now we can walk it.'

'Chivalry has broken out.'

'I should of course do my essay,' said Hubert.

'Ride on the crossbar of my bike. Bicyclary.' Tom laughed; others groaned.

'Perhaps our friend has a car, scientists being at a premium.'

'Ignore him,' said Manghan. 'Blasted Orton. Condescending bastard, aren't you, cock?'

'I'll walk you across. I mean if you want me to.' William had made the offer out of mechanical tact to de-fuse Dick's outburst, not that Orton seemed to mind. Now he became embarrassed himself.

'It isn't necessary,' she said, smiling (a smile that strangely pained him). 'I'm capable of going solo, even in Cambridge. Don't you sometimes feel you're living in the Ark?'

'All the time,' said Manghan. 'All the bloody time.'

'All right,' she said, switching back to him. 'Isn't it about ten miles?'

'It was a compromise between not having a station and having it half way to London. You know, Ruskin and Co.'

'That's interesting.' Manghan seemed to mean it and William was pleased to have met him on his own ground, or half way there.

As they crossed an area of trees and backwaters the mist drooped in remarkable ribbons lit by scattered lamps. Moistness and dark pegged equally.

'Stagey old Cambridge.' Janet stopped with a gesture. 'Just look at it.'

'I work here. I know Hubert and Co. do.'

'But they're undergraduates.'

83

'No. I've been here longer. It's like anywhere else.'

'Well, I'm not going to ask you about your work. That's too safe. Tom, Dick and Harry are not, you know, any old Tom, Dick and Harry, are they?'

'No. Hubert's rarer somehow. But he's your brother.'

'Do you find being related odd?'

'Us, do you mean?'

'People always ask me what I mean. Jack nearly drives me crazy.'

William was determined to protect her, if only from missing the train. He let Jack drift off unexplained and kept walking. She might be one who could talk only when standing still. Eventually he said, 'Family histories always sound made up.'

She sounded as if she'd been waiting for him to speak. 'Odder than when they're happening. It's because they happen slowly and get told in ten minutes.'

'Two for mine. Divorce and now one parent unheard of and my mother in Fréjus, South of France.'

'It's a shame, families splitting up but I don't see why it should be. Being related is very odd once you question it.'

'Apart from parthenogenesis it's unavoidable.'

She didn't reply—either because she knew the word and his wit tasted flat; or because she had no idea. His wit felt flat and he began to doubt the scintillation of Stanwick Street. The station was simply enormously far and he should have called a taxi.

'Is Manghan an aspiring poet?'

'What's that? I wouldn't know. Most of them end up writing for Beaverbrook.'

'Is that true?' she asked.

'No,' he said after a few steps, 'I don't suppose it is.'

'Poems are always about Life,' she complained, half to herself.

'Poets have to write about something.' His remark plopped into the black-breathing waters of the Cam by which they were now walking—or perhaps it was (more appropriately)

84

the Granta here; or even something else. 'The rollers,' he said. 'If you want to punt to Grantchester you pull the boat up here. There's still a couple of old men about who'll do it for you. I expect they remember palmier days and richer under-graduates.'

'They seem pretty rich now. And where else is palmy if this place isn't? Unless palmy was a pun.'

His regulation groan and her titter brought them suddenly close.

She claimed to know a short cut.

'We can cross over here.'

'This is shorter. Along the other way.'

'Grantchester for breakfast?'

'No, there's a footbridge. Really,' she said. 'And you who're supposed to have been here for years. It's further along.'

It was—much—and led into a part he hardly knew, a grove of very large houses in a maze of lanes.

She said: 'And a three-prongéd streetlamp shall be thy sign.'

It duly presented itself. She was triumphant.

'We're not there yet.'

'Through here.' They walked on a surface softened by fallen leaves. Looking at her feet, he wondered at the speed women made in high-heeled shoes, at women. They came to a dead-end at someone's garage—mossy, like a boathouse, nearly as old as the invention it held.

'It must be the other way,' said Janet. He was careful not to be satirical, partly because satire was not his style, partly out of consideration. Also it was unnecessary: 'I told you so' dripped from the air. Silently he pictured where they should be: well up Hills Road.

'Clever-Dick's lost herself.' Janet leaned against the Trinity street-lamp to which they had inexplicably returned.

'Try this one.' The only way left, it took them to a road he recognised. Now their feet rang on paving and they walked in the harsher separation of sodium lighting.

'I apologise for my short cut.'

A bus glimmered by, the driver of which, when flagged, slowed before changing mind and gears and sailing off. She went in for noiseless giggling and hung from a bus-shelter. 'Stitch.'

'It's nine-twenty. I'm a bit fast. It's possible.'

'Give me a piggy back.'

'If we try scout pace.'

'What's that?'

'You walk and then you run.'

'You run and I'll walk.'

'We *are* nearly there.' To him she seemed wilfully to be wasting time. The station, out on its scruffy limb, was visible. 'Try breathing.'

'Whatever for? I am breathing.'

'Deep breaths. You need oxygen.'

'I know that. I've got the stitch though.'

'Lactic acid.'

'Really?'

'You want oxygen to react with it.'

'Go on. What would that do?'

'Produce CO_2 presumably, which you could get rid of.'

'I'll try. You really are amazingly scientific.'

'You asked me. Can you go on?'

'Think so. Take my arm, Arthur.'

They got there. 'Two minutes in hand,' he said. 'Got a ticket?'

'Somewhere.'

The Spirit of British Railways at the barrier said: 'It's gone, if you wanted London.'

'We still do.' William put on his young don act, which wasn't his at all. 'It's not yet half past nine.'

'I never said it was.' The inspector sounded affable. 'Seeing she went out at 9.25, it doesn't matter.'

'What?'

'Re-timed because of Engineering. See the local press.'

86

'I don't read the local press. I only came this morning and it's Sunday.'

'Exactly, miss. In that case,' the inspector was becoming almost chatty, 'you should have seen the notices chalked up all over the station.'

'Preposterous.' William consulted his watch. 'When's the next?'

'Monday.'

'That's tomorrow.'

'That's correct, sir.'

'Is there a bus to London?'

'I've never heard of one.' The inspector looked at his own watch—grand enough to have been presented to George Stephenson—and walked away.

'This is serious.'

She said: 'Only mildly catastrophic.'

'Missing it like that.'

'It's spilt milk or split feet. I'm going to sit on these baskets. We missed it in style, didn't we?'

'What was all that about the local press?'

'It worries you. You just have to adjust to circumstances.'

'You sound like a Dutch Uncle,' he said, annoyed. He couldn't stop himself working out where they could have picked up five minutes—even four! Her short cut of course; but there was her stop at the bus shelter, her looking in a bookshop window ...

'You're much more like one. Perhaps it was pompous—I can be.' She sat neatly on a pigeon basket, black shoes together, dark hair lapping dark coat collar. In some way she was extracting cockeyed enjoyment.

He thought of taxis.

'To London?'

'Bishop's Stortford or somewhere. I could give a cheque.'

'I don't fancy Bishop's Stortford, I really don't.'

'What then? Hotel? I'll ring them.'

'It's a lot of trouble and I don't have the money.'

'There's my cheque-book.'

'Honestly, you're not paying, even if I pay you back—which I would of course. It seems such a lot of commotion. Almost middle-aged. I'll doss down in the waiting-room. There's bound to be an early train.'

'No you won't.' He was aghast. 'You can't,' he said.

'I've slept in all sorts of places, trees actually. One tree. I can't recommend them.'

'Look,' he said, 'it's not on.'

'I've caused you enough upset.'

'Let's start again.'

'Not Bishop's Stortford please.'

William knew her short cut would out in a minute, that it must be prevented. His agitation corroborated her comments on Cambridge the Ark. He was flustered. Gentlemanly attitudes hustled him to the one indisputable point: she could not doss down on the station. Even if the Railway permitted it, it was not in the nature of things.

'You might as well doss down at my place. Or why not Hubert's?'

'Yours then. Various reasons why not Hubert's. But aren't yours College and wouldn't the presence of Woman—me—bring the whole thing to its medieval knees?'

'I'm in digs.' College so much easier! Mrs Sugden's knees; the bloody canary screaming blue murder. But if not that it would be Bishop's Stortford third time round. God, why didn't he take things in his stride? A bus outside made up his mind. 'Let's get out of here.'

They re-covered the ground with threepenny ease. Top-deck conjunctions with bowls of huge cornflakes took them to the centre where they crawled cheek by jowl with half the heraldry of England, squint-eyed gateways, ancient castellated incubators of all the talents.

When the duffled head in front turned, it was Gore's. He stared. 'Goodyear.'

'Miss Anstey.' William embarked on introductions.

'Good.'

'Goodnight.' Gore extended a hand, withdrew it. He could

88

have been shaping himself for a proposal; instead he flung himself downstairs as the bus moved.

'Who on earth was that?'

'That was Gore.'

'Blimey. What does *he* do?'

'Insect Physiology.'

'I'm not surprised.' Janet shrugged deeper in her coat.

William caught one farewell sight of his colleague sprinting down King's Parade. True he was the most gauche, least successful presence imaginable—but the carpark revelations had flimsily bridged an old wide gap. Gore was human and perhaps ran now, so awkwardly as to knock himself over any minute, to escape. Whilst she shrugged, beautiful, untouched. Nonsense. Why was he gifting her with second sight?

'Magdalene Bridge,' he said—Cambridge being, after all, a tourist spot.

It was the first time the room of green mounds and iron umbrella had fetched a welcome out of him. Door and stairs had been managed without question, the canary staring itself in the beak.

'Good heavens, is this it?'

'Yes.' William felt unable to denounce his room, though it was hardly necessary to do so. It was a room standing up for itself, difficult to knock down—even a worthy contestant in Sugden vs. Taste. It was also, however much he detested it, his room. He could feel himself sinking with it. Some archaic tie of animal with lair was operative. Tugging uselessly at curtains, straightening absurd doilies, he realised that she was the first to have seen it. Gore had been invited for coffee once but had not arrived.

'There's the bedroom as well. They made it by partitioning. It's only big enough for the bed and doesn't have windows.'

'Arthur.' She was amused, even delighted. 'How horrible. Doesn't it do things to you, living in a place like this?'

'I haven't been in it long.'

'Won't it then? My London flat is a palace.'

89

'Aren't they expensive?'

'They are but this one belongs to Jack.'

'I see,' he said.

'Which means you don't. Have you noticed? "I see"—it's a sort of epitaph.'

'I don't see why.'

'Can you make coffee?'

'There's a gas-ring in the bathroom.'

He waited for the kettle to boil, a genuinely cheap and battered kettle. Once the bath, whose sides were permanently stained (acid perhaps—some previous Mr Sugden, after much steeping, down the plughole?), had contained the present Mr Sugden, the bolt having failed. There he was, a flannel over his penis so as not to embarrass himself, floating through some steaming novel—steaming. Mr Sugden, William reflected, could be the classic apple-core, pecked to apologetic shreds—or not. He didn't know. No real evidence had been forthcoming the few times they'd met; he had discreetly wiped himself from sight in face of the business being discussed—a tooth-paste tube not properly disposed of, a rebate. They lived separated by thin walls and floorboards, entirely.

She had taken her coat off when he got back.

'Any sign of the enemy?'

'It's ... ten past ten.' Swivelling his wrist to find out and almost, but not quite, depositing the tray (a tin thatched cottage)'s contents at her feet.

'Them I meant—the landlady. Not the time! Let me take that. "How goes the enemy?" Just like your Uncle George.'

'Step-father.'

'Yes. Fancy thinking of him at all.'

'Do you mean I imitate him or that I'm like him?'

'No, I didn't mean anything. I just said it. Sorry. Keep my voice down.'

'I don't see what they can say anyway. We're relations.'

'Taken in sin with a banned relative's worse. Are we banned? Just the stocks then instead of the stake.'

'They don't burn people in Cambridge.'

'I must have been thinking of Oxford.'

'They're thinking of stopping it there. You have the bed and I'll kip in here. The top drawer has clean pyjamas.'

'Lovely.'

'I'll watch whilst you wash.'

'Watch whilst I wash?'

'Perhaps be a bit quiet.'

'I shan't wash. I never do.'

'Erm ...' She had opened the bedroom door with unprecedented din; then popped her head out to say: 'At least we won't have to worry about the noise of bedsprings.'

That unnecessary remark was what he was left with. Still, it was not Gore's prerogative to make sudden, miscalculated remarks. She meant nothing by it. He was unembarrassed, cold—when that morning the idea of a girl (half-cousin admittedly) in his bed (himself not in it, admittedly) would have been fantasy, if that. Yet, like the remark, he was left in the air.

Under the crinoline of the mad Victorian lady he found his cigarettes. There was one left, weeks or months old. Bent in two places, it reminded him of Abraham Lincoln. The link was elusive. When lit it leaked half way down. William surveyed himself in the convex mirror surrounded by iron vine leaves. Anyone looked like a frog in it. Unsuccessful smoke wisped in the room.

During the night Meteorology asserted itself by hacking off degrees and pulling fronts like curtains. Cambridge glittered with frost beneath a rinsed blue sky.

He had seen the morning in. The leather settee and leather armchair covered again in green grew innocuous in the light of day. He had tried lying on the settee with his shins at right-angles on the chair, but the chair had moved slowly away; he had tried sleeping with his shoulder on the chair and his body at right angles on the settee. He came to on the floor almost with gratitude for having slept. The grey tussle with the night was over; in his bed Janet lay in slumber and he tried to get some comfort at the thought. Well before seven he was watching the gas-ring. Pipes grumbled and growled at him. When he tapped on his own door and opened it she sat up at once, his jacket strange on her and falling wide to show most of a breast. She came to as bright as the sky. 'Tea—smashing!'

'If we go out at half past Mrs Sugden's always doing her ablutions then—she takes at least ten minutes. I'll leave a notice cancelling my breakfast and we'll get some on the way.'

'If you think all that's necessary.'

'You know,' he said hopelessly. 'If you want to use the bathroom I should now. They don't get up for fifteen minutes.'

She swung out of bed, managing a marginal modesty in his pyjama jacket. Noticing too late as it were the tasselled trousers folded at the end of the bed, he jumped back. She was out for what seemed fifteen minutes but was probably five. He pictured a meeting on the landing: Mrs Sugden in her Boer War dressing-gown and Janet.

But Janet came back dressed. '*The Diary of Anne Frank*. We now listen for Mrs S to move in?'

'Yes.'

'You'll end up being taken away—or your head in that gas-ring.'

When he carelessly mentioned the young gentleman, she wanted to know more. Everyone did—Earwaker, even Gore. The canary got them every time.

'Don't build them up.' She was serious, as if she cared about it. 'You know—ignore them.' He was tired and anxious to get the cold but safe air of outside in their nostrils. At half-past the bathroom door gave them warning. At the foot of the stairs they encountered Mrs Sugden who, transparent duster in hand, lunged out from the lounge. The canary buzzed.

In his hand William had the breakfast note. Startled, she took it.

'So it won't be breakfast?'

'My cousin,' he said.

'Cold.'

'But fine.'

The trees flanking his genuinely short cut were dressed overall with frost. 'That's "The Wedding Cake"—St John's.' He was an expert guide. Two years had passed since he'd taken his mother round, a day weighted like lead in his memory.

'It's beautiful.'

'The style's early Gothick—with a k.'

'I'm glad I stayed. It's beautiful. English perfection. A marvellous place.'

'One of its better days,' he admitted.

But not for breakfast. There was not a crumb to be had and the first train shuffled in on an empty stomach.

'Longest platform in England. I know why but I've forgotten.'

'Royalty?' She was vague.

'I say, is there a buffet car?' he asked a passing porter, who passed. Small crowds blustered round. Without luggage to manhandle, he held the door. Janet poked out her dark head. 'Don't wait. Just a minute. This is the London address.'

'I'll keep in touch with Hubert.'

'Just a second.' She drew him near enough with the paper to land a kiss. 'You've been sweet.'

He gestured with an arm awkwardly and cleared the barrier.

'Sweet' seemed an amazing accolade. He walked it back to the college amongst an increasing density of the rooks of learning. All when he should have been stumbling on Goodyear's First Law of Energy Conversion.

A pigeonhole note sent him after breakfast to fill in for someone at another college and, whether it was the room pleasantly overlooking a frosty garden of centuries' tending in place of the usual broom-cupboard lab, the coming of coffee on a salver, or something in his mood, he had never been so brilliant. He lunched on the strength of it and in the afternoon juggled his figures into such a dazzle they looked like results. Even returning in mid-evening he greeted Mrs Sugden without a qualm. Washing, he found his pyjama jacket hanging undisturbed on the bathroom door. He buried his face and

93

arms in it before the sketchy electric fire—to keep warm, but perhaps a little as if to stem pints of blood flowing out of him. The green mounds wouldn't cheat his sleep tonight but the iron light began again to stab.

TWO

At first he didn't recognise her, or only with effort. Tricia, of course, took up the point. 'Little boy lost,' she said quite brightly. 'You would pick this Tube, you always do. It's got sixty exits.'

'New costume?'

'Costume? You're a generation out of date. Two-piece.'

'Striking.' He was trying to spike the inevitable. All the way from Cambridge he'd been preparing himself not to re-act as he always did react to his sister. Which is to say that in odd minutes between reading and countryside—yes, and looking at Janet's address—he had. By appearing like this, she had made his preparation inadequate. By any measure she looked absurd—the thick pink costume, the scraped hair, the green make-up. How should she be? An old raincoat, a differ-ent face, the little sister she wasn't? Men seemed to notice her, if London men noticed anything, one brushing her there and then by accident and his hunted London face blossoming an apology she smile-fully returned. 'Well,' she said mollified. 'How are the worms?'

'How are you?' It came out a little unfortunately, for she had opinions of his idea of her; their relationship was a quick-sand of everything except tenderness. Caradoc, arriving sud-denly, saved further early disintegration. A ten-ton truck, parping with rage, hissed off down Earls Court Road.

Caradoc was new to him, but unmistakable. His face, nest-ing in whiskers and hair looked up from an impossible hori-zontal and the shiny red Mini seemed packed with him. 'Hop in.'

William gladly volunteered for the back—one of his minor,

previously unrealised reluctances was talking sideways to people, especially to strangers. 'Fine.'

Caradoc guided Tricia's hip. She clunked the door to on its pull-rope, frustrating the catch.

'Map-bin, miss,' Caradoc leaned over the pink lap, the frissoning thighs. It was a fussy thing, said unfussily.

'Sorry,' she said. 'I'm used to the old one.'

From his small grandstand he noticed the details, her play-acting particularly. 'The old one'—she turned as they went off, Caradoc, forehead to steaming windscreen, brain on the rush-hour—'was a real snorter. Riley?'

'The old Riley? Real bomber.'

'It was a gem but it was dipso about petrol.'

'Fabric body,' said Caradoc, reprieved by traffic lights.

'Caddy was the only one who could make it go. I'm taking lessons with BSM. I don't suppose you drive, Willy. It's such a long time, isn't it? I wonder sometimes what you do up there, apart from your worms.'

Caradoc said: 'You remember that thing once called the Diet of Worms? Still tickles me.'

'A certain schoolboy humour.'

William knew he had manufactured half his headache about her on the ride down but here she was subtly siding with him against Caradoc—hers was a superiority she had to share for it to exist—but typically passing it off as something quite different, the conventional banter of loving wife or practical guardian of whiskery genius—even of subordinate will. He hated knowing all this, imagining all this. He fiercely rubbed mist off Triplex to look at the muck outside. Look again, Charity, see something else, something new. Tricia was a woman now and they'd never been close. And no generalising, no random sample of one: women were not a species.

Caradoc did things round bollards—there was hooting but they were through, driving steeply. Now he had simple country bumpkin—complex country bumpkin—admiration of wheel-spinning Caradoc of whom London turned not a hair.

96

'Dripping evergreens,' said Caradoc. 'Everblacks. What do you think of us? Behold our rustic foot of earth. The old woman below told me there was a nightingale in that tree when she first came here.'

'Delusions of Berkeley Square.' Tricia held up the seat for him to extricate himself. Even that action to his disgust he registered: forcep-fingered Tricia extracting one brother.

'Swish place,' he said. 'You zoom about. Do you remember that nice basement place in Kilburn?'

'God, you are out of date. There's been Chalk Farm and common Clapham. Still, it's nice to think there's someone who finds our pace smart.'

Another question—did that mask some sort of affection or did she literally mean it—metropolitan simple-mindedness? Following up the stairs, many and grand, something in him trembled more like a last everblack leaf than last, nerve-wrecked nightingale. The Mini had bounced him; London, Tricia, Caradoc had bounced him. Faint and useless, he was ushered into the flat.

'Do comment.' Tricia was already in a flouncey housecoat. 'We've spent every penny and every minute.'

'It's marvellous.'

'Think so?' Caradoc glowed.

'The colours ... did you do that ceiling?'

'He is a painter, quite gifted. I'll make coffee whilst you two men etcetera.' She went through a door done in white and orange.

'You can see it's irregular—we've got one of the bays. 1920 —just when no one knew where the hell they were. I had to locate the centre of the biggest possible circle to leave white and do the rest with that deep orange. Commercial paint with added pigment.'

'Did you use string?'

'Trial and error? No, I did a scale drawing and used compasses. Trig, more or less. You see there was one spot, one centre. It was exactly where I thought, judging by eye. But you can no longer judge by eye.'

'I thought you said you did?' William found himself perfectly relaxed.

'Coincidence. There's always the Idea but human instinct's played out. Besides, there's no such thing.'

'We have instincts.'

'Your subject,' said Caradoc. 'Excuse me, you're treading on my subject. I am an animal.' He scratched his beard. 'And to prove it I'm hair. Yackaboo.'

William laughed. 'Your word. The species extends to culture. It's not unique there either. Ecology is a coming thing.'

'I ought to know what it means then. What's my line? A shop-floor Culture worker. That's what I mean. As we trek bravely into the 1960s we've got to abandon our baggage, a lot of which is Culture, judging by eye included. I've been reading this book.'

William nodded indulgently. No one in the SCR admitted to having read a book. Most of them had read a great number but they were Tilth there; here in the city books scurried along the paving to be seized.

'Burroughs?' Caradoc put in an almost transatlantic question mark.

'That's the name of my adding-machine.'

'He's related, I think. He's important because he sees what we are.'

'What he thinks we are.'

'I admire academics. What he thinks we are—but he's really chucked illusion. He's part of something new.'

'I've not read it.'

'You should—I'd lend it to you, except that someone's got it already. That's a point.'

'I'll wait for the film then.'

'You'd have to wait a long time.'

'I'm sorry about the chairs.' His sister came with the coffee perfectly arranged on a tea-trolley graceful as Chippendale.

'What chairs, mate? She means she's sorry for the lack of chairs.'

98

'Sucks.'

'Caught off your brother then. He pulled me up.'

'You need pulling up,' said Tricia. 'I mean that literally.'

'How about that for a remark?' Caradoc shuffled baffled round the bay-window. 'How about that?'

'We decided to get good stuff. Once you fill the place with any old junk you get used to it. Classic question: do you take sugar?'

'Two,' said William.

'Classic answer,' said Caradoc. 'You see, Tricia said I was a painter. I was.' He seemed to have got over the jolt, whatever it had been. 'It's correct to the extent that I've been through one of the better-known Art Schools. All those still-lifes and still alive! One-man shows, the man being the hired attendant. Private booze. "The reticence of his treatment is quietly alarming." The whole notion of Art has gone down the drain. You can hear the bugger gurgling.'

'I can see it must be difficult.'

'He doesn't mean he's given up,' Tricia explained. 'He means *it's* given up. William doesn't claim to know about art. I think it's style. Caddy has his uses. We know some rather key people between us.'

'And she doesn't mean the Nine Worthies like you have at your place.'

'Now I'm lost.'

'Little boy lost.' Tricia's wit, loaded and obvious always, bounced lightly off him.

'You're putting me up. Let me get you a meal. I'll squander my stipend. Do you like Indian?'

It repeated as they climbed back up the stairs with tropical mouths and feet like ice-floes. Tricia found something on the door. 'A note.'

After the restaurant the room looked completely unfurnished and felt cold. 'What's in that note?'

'Let me get in,' she said, laughing. 'It may be for Wilhelm. You help me wash up, Willy, and we can talk.'

'Pay *and* wash up,' said Caradoc. 'I tell you these days women want to eat their cake and have it.' He threw a chance slap which caught her roundly on the buttock.

'That was *quite* convincing.' She made a private face. 'Perhaps curry is the answer.'

'Curry my favours. Gerroff.' And Caradoc who hadn't paid went into the bedroom, showing no sign of washing up.

'Hold a tea-towel and look intelligent. Lunch, breakfast *and* last night.'

'Three generations,' said William.

'You like the flat?'

'Superb. He's got taste. So have you, I mean.'

'Flair—he has. And contacts. The Design thing's bound to happen. We can't walk about for ever dressed like the Queen Mum. And, my sweet, we mean to be in on it. You'd had wind of Caddy?'

'Quite a description on your Xmas card. I recognised the beard.'

'That may come off. I don't know yet.' She turned an eager look. 'You're not—what's the word—shocked? Co-habitation's all the rage. If it's not man and girl it's girl and girl or man and man and—you know.'

He said he did. She turned out plates at speed, hot and wreathed in Sqezy. Wiping carefully, he could hardly keep pace: doing his bit to stop Sqezy passing along the food-chain.

'Heard anything of Daddy Dear?'

There had been the Christmas card, signed 'Your father' and stamped 'EC 4' by the GPO.

'Must look him up,' she said. 'Not that he'd be on the phone—more likely on meths.'

'We don't know.' Family emergency.

'Is *that* why you came? Go about peeping into strangers' faces—"Excuse me, you wouldn't be my father?"'

'What makes you cruel?'

'Me? Adjusting to circumstances isn't cruel.' Tricia washed her hands, neat as a surgeon. 'That's what life's about, Willy.

100

In one department Caddy's learning that. Don't ask me which.'

'I wouldn't.'

'You wouldn't. I've managed to digest the note. Cousin Janet's having a party. Asks you specially. You met in Cambridge, didn't you? It also turns out Jack has business with Caddy. So London really is the village we all say.'

He kept as much out of their way as possible in the one unfurnished room whilst they had it out who would stay in. The unseen bedroom might have harboured a sleeping baby of Caradoc's; even—with her casualness this last year or so— of hers. But it was Principle, Caradoc revealed on the stairs: one of their principles—not to go to parties together.

'Sensible arrangement,' said Caradoc.

Agreeing, he wondered why. But the fiddly cross-stitch of indoors was smothered by the snow which had come down suddenly the size of banknotes, redeeming a hundred million recent Xmas cards. Windscreen wipers whirred against it. People slipping from pavements giggled like children. Cars began to skid. So sudden.

'Monte or bust.' Caradoc purred in his beard; the journey was exciting.

William suggested a bottle of wine. Somehow he had missed imbibing any vinoculture whilst imbibing the wines themselves, especially at High Table. Not for the first time he realised that the possibilities of a brilliant academic career were limited. So he paid and Caradoc chose (thoughtfully) something at eight shillings.

'Hope the drink situation's all right,' said Caradoc. 'This we trust never to see again but may end up dolefully staring at: the last of the booze. By then quality's the last consideration.'

The party was upstairs and going like a party.

Someone doing the drinks made him their special concern and he soon felt on a par with a large Nigerian in magnificent tribal dress. 'How's Independence?'

The large Nigerian was related to the Speaker in Lagos and provided a guided tour—Westminster democracy blooming and secure. But William had discussed it before. A few facts and names made the Nigerian's smile more knowing. He laughed; now they were sharing a joke. The question or two William wanted answered was allowed to float off into the cigarette smoke.

The large Nigerian. The tubby nurse.

No one was with her though she knew someone who was working on a fabulous colour magazine they were going to *give away* with a newspaper and he was coming, only he hadn't.

William offered the snow, which she gratefully received; but soon she was telling him she was too fat. It was that, not the snow. 'I know they both melt but mine doesn't. What do you advise? There's the Middle East, isn't there? But if I went it would be service nursing and, you know, they don't let you talk to the natives and anyway the natives you'd want to talk to are all driving super Mercedes and wouldn't talk to you. There's no way out if you're fat.'

He denied it and the conversation settled on it. Tubbiness was her one subject. After twenty minutes she said confidentially: 'You know, I can talk about it with you. My problem,' she added fondly. But he had admitted to having no car, to trudging an ill-paid academic track. She wanted someone with transport, 'It doesn't have to be a sportscar but I don't mind them'—someone out of a coloured advertisement. Inside her fat she was comfortable and secure and William found he knew the notice on her door only too well—DO NOT DISTURB. But he was surprised—he liked her.

Caradoc and others sat together in a corner under a mushroom cloud of talk. He hung about on the fringes. 'Let me get the Edwardian bastard alone for five minutes and I'd punch his teeth down his throat.'

'Of course the Soviets have to arm. I'm for the Soviets.'

He had seen Janet early on before the Nigerian and she had rushed up between the Nigerian and the nurse. Now for the first time she was unbesieged, idly standing up some dried reeds in a vase.

102

'Is this where you live?'

'Hullo. Plush, isn't it? I saw Tricia in Marshall and Snel-grove, not that I usually go there—it was for someone else, Jack's aunt. She was rather surreptitiously sketching a dress. I whispered in her ear and she nearly jumped out of her coat. I was surprised: they don't have the sort of dresses she does. I'm sorry. You can't know anybody. There's all sorts—politics, lawyers, the lot. Now you—a don.'

'I wouldn't say that.'

'What? You have to. We don't go in for fine distinctions. "This is my Cousin Arthur—he's doing absolutely brilliant things in Cambridge. Do tell us what absolutely brilliant things you're doing." '

'The biomass of the insects in a woodland floor.'

' "But how super." Seriously, as they say round here, what's that?'

'Biomass? It's the idea of the total living matter in a given environment. The total biological weight. You know, for every cow in a field there's half a ton of earthworms under-neath. Earthworms are not my line.'

'So all of us here are the biomass?' She gestured with both arms, dark hair up, coming astray. He noticed she had shaved hair from her armpits and prized that. And either she was bitter or tired. He said the room was stuffy.

'I'll show you the balcony. Everywhere has to have a feat-ure. Like your lampshade. You still there? I'll tell you a secret: our balcony's on the back. The other houses that have them have theirs on the front. So the man who built it was eccentric or the view was better in 1882. You should have seen the view in 1882. We go through here. The biomass seems all right. This sticks.'

Yanking at the door, he felt the warmth of her naked arms and took off his jacket, lumpy with all sorts of junk and draped her in it.

'Heat loss.'

She protested.

'Take it from me—Medicine is only a branch of zoology.'

103

He opened the door with a similar flourish.

Janet went through, leaving footprints. The balcony was obviously the roof of part of the ground-floor flat, its railing more 1930 than 1882. She had no shoes on.

Thoughtfully closing the door, he turned to see her staring down into the garden, arms folded in his coat. One or two snowflakes settled on her head. 'What about shoes?'

'My feet don't get cold. I kicked them off to dance.'

'Everyone's do.'

'I get cold feet about the Bomb and about things like that. You can't talk. Where's your jacket?'

'I'm wearing a string vest.'

'Prove it. I'm going abroad next week—icy Copenhagen. Jack's going. That's why I am. It must be nice being a zoologist. I still like the zoo. I suppose that doesn't count. Nice to have a rest from people. You see everyone tied up in their circumstances and you know them and they have to suffer all the appropriate feelings, emotions. I don't know what I mean. Too much feeling perhaps.'

He knew she was being serious. Her feet hurt him extraordinarily.

'There won't in your feet.'

'What did Mrs Thing say? I forgot to ask.'

'Mrs Sugden? Nothing much, nothing at all.'

'*Carte blanche* to bring in all the Cambridge tarts.'

'Not really.' That had pained him, too.

'You must have some social life. You can't work all the time in the lab.'

'At least half in the field.'

'Ha ha.'

'There's a jazz club. I went with a friend the other day. He wants to marry. I'm not sure he didn't propose. I'm trying to forget it.'

'I wish Jack had been here for you to meet, but he's gone already to wonderful, wonderful Copenhagen.'

'Your feet. You'll get double pneumonia.'

'One in each foot. Perhaps I want to. How about that?

So that I shan't have to go to Denmark. That sounds as hopeless as it is—anyway I'm not sure I don't want to go. Danes are all right in their place and Copenhagen's their place. What does fresh air do to alcohol?'

'I can't think it's oxidised or anything.'

'Stitch,' she said.

'Circulation?'

'My circulation is increasing. Millions! Cold feet, warm head. Arthur, you may carry me over the threshold.'

Without hesitation, he took her up on it, one arm round her back, the other hand sliding up stocking onto warm leg so that he had her weight—but somehow athwart. She saved herself by an adroit shift. His jacket slid overboard, spattering change.

'Wow,' said someone when they got inside, William backing.

'We were children together.' She threw herself into a careless horizontal; William staggered. 'It's true,' she said.

Behind her eyes, what? Pain, desperation? Fleeting—unmeasurable.

'I can't go back in there.' She landed on the carpet. 'I'll get these wet things off.' Slipping up her hem, she released the stockings and rolled them off. He saw nothing in that. Now he had her eyes to worry him as well as her feet. 'I want to talk to you. This flat's disgustingly huge. It isn't but I always say it is. It's quite large. See, I deny everything I say these days. If you don't mind a bedroom. It will be warm: the latest and best paraffin heater that glugs like a frog. You probably want a drink.'

'No.'

'It'll look compromising if anyone notices. They all do, this lot. Up here.'

'It's the nearest thing we've got to an attic.'

She pushed hard on the door and switched on the light. Immobile beneath it Caradoc and the tubby nurse more or less unclad—Caradoc in all his hairiness, the nurse in all her tubbiness, doing nothing as yet, still undoing everything.

105

'God!' Janet felt round for the lightswitch. 'Why didn't you bolt the door? There's a perfectly good bolt.' She extinguished the expressionless faces and slammed the door to.

'Your sister's boyfriend. I bet it gets through to her. All I wanted to do was talk. Glug, glug—a comfortable background noise.'

Half way down again, she stopped, forehead touching the wall, laughing.

'What is it?'

'Thinking,' she said. 'We always seem to be witnessing copulations.'

He knew what she meant. It struck him like something long forgotten, a summons, an arrest. She went on laughing, weakly and softly. He could have struck her then and perhaps she sensed it, looking up. But there she was, the evidence before him. Suddenly he changed again. 'Stop.'

And she stopped. 'It's not hysterics. It's nothing. It's an off-day. I'm sorry. I want to dance. Come on.'

THREE

'Whose idea was this?' Jack for a certainty advanced with outstretched hand.

William popped in his. 'Yours?' But Jack with time for only a squirt of laughter, not unattractive, meaning anything, was off to some crisis of Stores.

They were all there, the whole lot—but more like survivors brought ashore than prospective sailors of the Norfolk Broads. He caught sight of Hubert on one of the yachts. Tricia flared in red, white and blue: a highly unserviceable ransacking of the world's navies. Caradoc was more like it, more like the grey day and William drifted over. On the way he had his gaberdine tweaked by Tricia. 'Trust you,' was all she said.

'The man said the transom won't take an outboard. I said it was bloody typical. He didn't deny it. *He just walked off.*' Roger, by a process of elimination. Unless this was Jack. Somehow he knew through knowing Janet the first one was Jack.

Standing there, William felt in full flood those tepid uncertainties lapping him on the train. They were feelings he had had before, often enough at school, once on the eve of his National Service medical (failed on the mildest of hay fevers). Neotenic then. Tricia right to pick on the raincoat: her flair always to pick on something.

'Seen Janet?'

'On a boat.' Caradoc was as dismal as last time, after that party way back in the winter.

'Oughtn't we to be doing something?'

'I'm doing it. Freezing.'

'Haven't you done something to your beard?'

'Mutton chops.' Caradoc took an interest. 'They're coming on, aren't they? Modelled on all those Victorian geysers. We've got the nineteenth century all wrong, know that? Especially the Pre-Raphs; you'll be hearing more of the Pre-Raphs. All we've been doing is reacting like old Lytton Strachey, taking the foul old creep for gospel when it stands out a mile he had a castration complex. Refer to Freud. Eliot and all those pussy-foots have distorted the whole bloody period.'

William was reluctantly impressed by Caradoc's 'sincerity' as much as the dropped names.

Janet appeared in a cockpit with another girl. She was waving a tin.

'Who brought frogs' legs? We can get those fresh.'

'There's nothing, but simply nothing like messing about in boats.'

'Sarah—William, my forty-second cousin. Have you met Roger and Jack? Hubert's just gone off to the post office about two miles away. At least I think so.' She jumped neatly down. Old jeans, floppy pullover, bare feet. 'Have you found the tap?'

Tricia—so opposite—shook her carefully got-up head and yawned. It was a familiar yawn, as wide as the boatyard.

William said he'd look.

'No, you've just arrived. Come and see the boats. Holidays like this are supposed to be relaxing. Of course they aren't. If they work at all it's like Electric Shock Treatment. The only thing is not to let them get you down.'

'When do we sail?'

'I don't know. How are you though?'

'Is this one of ours?'

'The *Stella*—four berths and auxiliary motor. These two are Shrikes, "fast, sporty craft for the experienced yachtsman." How fast, sporty or experienced are you?'

'I'm not,' he said. 'Bits of rock-climbing.'

'Now it's raining. Come into this Shrike. Mind your head. It's not always as low as this. You lift the lids when you

108

moor and it's all mod cons—gas, electricity and a lavatory somewhere. What are they called on ships? Bulkheads?'

'Just heads, I think.' They crouched in the saloon.

'We haven't allocated ships. I know that sounds like Jack, but each boat needs a skipper. He's insistent on that and no doubt right. So it becomes intriguing—who goes with whom, especially on these Shrikes. I can't seem to get any sense out of Tricia and Caradoc I thought wasn't coming. He doesn't look nautical. Roger and Sarah have both undoubtedly won cups. Hubert can only punt, according to him, but he's young enough to learn. I told him with John flying jets he ought to be able to manage one of these things. Don't say it—it's all a terrible mistake. Actually it's like a desert island or snow-girt mansion—you know, a controlled experiment.'

'Only not controlled.'

'Imagine a week of it.'

The old salts—or peats—of the boatyard, when found, kept calm. The only sailing advice they gave was when one of them acquiesced in Roger's forecast of using the quanting-pole. 'This reach of the Bure's well wooded as I remember,' said Roger, then with wetted finger—'Light airs.' 'You can't beat the old pole,' was the actual response. Every week a jittery batch of Nelsons to send downstream!

In the fore peak of *Stella* William's berth was the oddest of the lot. You fed yourself into a door marked 'R.I.P.' by some previous hirer and there you were with a few cigar-box shelves to keep your things on and one porthole against madness. In a way it suited him ... too well. By the light of a tiny bulb he unpacked—washing and reading matter, after-shave with an American schooner on it, a new paperback, *Culture and Society*, which he must have brought to prime him for conversation with Caradoc. Somehow he foresaw conversations with Caradoc and Tricia skulking in the background. They would never get through the week *en masse*—pairings would take place. But most were paired already: Roger and Sarah, his sister and Caradoc ... Janet and Jack.

109

Hubert and himself were the only spares, so why hadn't he looked forward to the more pleasing prospect of walks to pubs with Hubert? Why these fated, unwanted talks with Caradoc? That snapshot of him and the nurse caught with their pants down? Not possibly. Was falling asleep. Watery grave.

Had. Distinctly into his head which he had left on something hard, which was all creased, came authentic sounds of water chuckling under the prow. It gurgled like a new bottle of sherry. *Stella* was under way and everything hitherto thought or half thought about himself, Janet, Caradoc, this holiday, was academic from this moment. Academic, it was useless!

He scrambled out but stopped to get rid of his raincoat and put on squash shoes. He emerged up a few steps amidships. The weather was brighter and there was a breeze, though nightfall was not far off. *Stella* seemed to be sailing crisply, heeled over a few degrees and on a tight rein. 'Hi!' Janet waved from the cockpit where she balanced in a straight line against the gunwale. He waved back. 'We thought you'd gone to sleep.'

'Think I did.' He walked carefully along the high-riding side. Like this, *Stella* was transformed, marvellous. He had never been under sail. Masterly Jack was at the tiller—a pipe going, which he smoked with great ease, at regular intervals dropping smoke which held together, dipped over the stern and spread richly on the clucking, glassy Bure.

Choosing one of the few places looking foolproof, William sat down.

'She may jib on this next bend. Duck if she does.'

'You should have got me to help.'

'Why?' Jack asked the question straight but didn't follow it up.

'Better out of the way? You're probably right.'

'Don't think that. Necessary charade sort of thing. You talk, Janet—I'm only making noises. Feeling how she sails.'

Janet made a face. 'Have a good nap?'

'Terrible. I wasn't even tired.'

'Oxidisation,' she said. 'We've left the others standing. Roger's teaching Tricia and Caradoc; Hubert's sitting at the feet of Sarah. Jack says we're better off for being taller, because of the trees.'

'The absence of trainees helps.'

'And the absence of trainees helps. I believe if there was a dead calm he could blow it along, couldn't you, Jack?'

'Probably have to,' he said. 'Small marine engines are bad enough at the best of times, but small diesel engines of unknown parentage look to me like a real bastard.'

'What about those houses though?' They reached their gardens down to the water's edge, some with neat boathouses and others raggeder, making intricate geography for children.

'Water rats,' said Jack.

'*Wind in the Willows*. I loved that book.'

'Money,' said Jack. 'Great Norwich merchants or what?'

'No idea.' William felt the remark had been addressed to him. 'Could be retired professors with consultancies.'

'That's your line, isn't it?'

'More a pure scientist.'

'I like that.' Jack let out more smoke, more rope. He had a facility for being elusive: it was hard to know what his remarks implied, if anything. His presence was relaxed, authoritative. William was puzzled.

The circumstances favoured odd remarks that slipped easily away; they were quietly, generally favourable. Called in he suspected as a makeweight, William had a comfortable immunity. He was a passenger, not even under training. All he lacked was his pipe, stowed below, and he could watch for ever the bank gliding expertly by and look out for the change to the real peatland of the Broads, possibly the odd swallowtail, rarer calcicoles amongst the *Phalaris* grass. He had Janet's concern for family relationships to thank, he supposed. As they moved with the rightness claimed by sailing men his confidence became serene; he nearly said, 'this is the life'. A sinking sun and the rapid dispersal of cloud produced a special clarity of light which isolated objects, but softly, endowing

them with distinctness and repose. Evidence of connection between the other two was hard for his observer's eye to make
out and he rested it. The minutes were a sample of timeless-
ness; they and the *Stella* were instantly fitted into the turn
of the moment, hung balancing along the Bure.

When Jack said, 'She's going,' William jumped lightly to his
feet. The sail had changed into a gibbering monster on a pole.
He looked to Jack to see where he should go, believing there
would be one spot, one movement to that spot to make his
weight part of the required manoeuvre. The push did not seem
a random blow and he dropped overboard without much belief
in what had occurred. His ears came out hearing nothing of
his own splash but only the flapping of canvas as the boat
went away and a shout, or a couple of shouts, of laughter. He
tried to shout back. He had some quite witty remark, but lost
it. A green chunk of water filled his mouth. He was being
dipped, he thought, dipped and pulled up. Either he was
laughing or spitting out water, which ran in again. Aware of
weed, long and rooted in the river-bed his feet could not find,
unbelieving, he began to drown.

His limbs fought for him whilst his mind watched. Of all
the things he'd acquired swimming not being one seemed
ironic.

He may have lost consciousness, or not. He was face-down
in a little creek with someone pumping on his backbone. That
was artificial respiration—kind but unnecessary of them.
Their kindness was overwhelming. Tears as well were coming
out of him. He was a little child trying to say sorry. They
stopped pumping. Nausea climbed up inside, a great sul-
phurous taste. Unsuccessfully, he was sick. The retching was
terrible but in the sweetness of survival his absolute weakness
flowed gently through him. Hands helped him. Helping them,
he sat up.

'We thought you were fooling.' Jack stood against the sky
with a boathook, like a pikeman. It was Janet propping him,
as wet as he was.

'Really quite graceful,' she said. 'That stuff about "going

down for the third time" mayn't be scientific but we didn't risk it.'

'I'll moor her then if she hasn't gone.'

'Get a kettle on. Can you walk? God knows where the towels are—on one of the Shrikes, I expect.' She pulled off her sweater, which seemed to hold gallons. 'I should have warned you—the jib or boom or whatever it is is the one thing to watch out for.'

'I'm sorry. I've set myself up as the ship's idiot.'

'It's not as bad as that. Ships have cats anyway. Villages have idiots.' She laughed. 'You didn't waste much time though.'

'You'll get cold,' he said for the very obvious reason she had on only a brassiere and soaking jeans and because he still saw her, Jack, anyone through the eyes of a survivor—tentatively solicitous of their matchless welfare.

'Our relationship seems to consist of you saying that … and me being said that to. Which is how you talk when you muff a gerund.'

'I seem to have muffed everything.'

The Shrikes arrived separately. The first bore Caradoc, Tricia and Roger and made its landfall under a cloud of mutual speechlessness. Tricia spoke first—no one else did—and then only to say, 'My God, what a prospect.' By now the Bure was darkening and the life of it both waking with plops and sleeping with silence under the impetus of dusk. The crew of the *Stella* (Jack's lanterns on the boom, Janet's cocoa) had done their best for the arrivals—but Roger had only just been coaxed from minutely swarming over his vessel as if decontaminating it—when the others floated in.

'Mainsail in. Hard aport.' Hubert's voice floated across.

'It's jolly diff to judge in this light.'

'Can't you reverse?'

'Not an earthly.'

Voices across still water indeed had a special quality—long-distance, limpid, oddly remote. In *Stella's* cockpit, all gloom and cocoa, they registered with at least two of them. Janet said to her cocoa 'Good old Hubert' and William—who had categorised Sarah on sight—moved to the same thought. Hubert did not seem to categorise at all and the private accord on the incoming boat touched William with envy, envy without malice as if he was two generations older.

'Cocoa's the right thing,' said Hubert, landing. 'Don't you think it is, Sarah?'

'Rather,' came Sarah's voice from the reeds.

'I smelt it. Hullo. Sorry about being so long. We got stuck.'

'*He* fell in,' said Tricia, which was all she knew about it so far.

'It's easy to fall in. In fact I fell overboard.'

'He did.' Sarah followed him with shining face. 'It was in a cornfield! We were aground, you see, so gently we hadn't felt her go. Hubert uttered this wildly appropriate shriek and there he was up to his knees in it.'

'We nearly killed ourselves getting it—her—back in.'

'Yes, and we'd never have at all if that old reed-cutter hadn't come along.'

'Good job he did.'

'He was a marvellous old man, a real reed-cutter. It's how he gets his living. Honestly. Do you know what they use the reeds for?'

'I can guess.' Caradoc spoke low from a corner.

'What?' Sarah hung like a rocky plum.

Caradoc must have been depending on silence as a reply, but in the unaccustomed surroundings, the lamp's pool of chumminess, the great expedition atmosphere, it wasn't answering. 'To make nests for reed-buntings,' he said eventually.

'That's ridiculous...!'

William found himself talking about Wicken Fen, the most documented and one of the earliest of nature reserves. He sketched its history from the early misconceptions of what was natural, what man-made; explained the process of re-colonisation by bur-reed and reedmace; and culminated with

114

an announcement that reed- and peat-cutters had literally made the Norfolk Broads. That he had done it and that it was complete news to them equally surprised him.

The pub was crowded: fleets of yachtsmen and motor-boaters —the yachtsmen with difficulty exploiting their superiority, sailors being by tradition taciturn—and a number of locals, none of whom (in the Saloon Bar at least) remotely resembled a reed-cutter.

William waited at the bar to get a brandy for himself and a sea of beer for the others. Someone had beaten him to it with an even mightier order and he was studying the quasi-obscene pokerwork mottoes behind the bar. 'Hullo.' Janet by his side in a pink dress, tight in the bodice but full in the skirt, shoulders bare. Tricia had changed into something extra-ordinary with pieces of fur; Sarah had come as she was. 'The experiment's under way,' said Janet.

'I thought we'd agreed it wasn't.'

'I was forgetting. Can't you just have an experiment though and see what happens?'

'No, you see if what you think will happen does—you test an hypothesis.'

'Which makes it sound limited.'

'It is,' he said. 'It extends itself when you revise your hypo-thesis.'

'What's your current thesis?'

'About what?'

She studied him, amused. 'You, for instance.'

'The same as usual. Unrevised.'

'Hm. The ship's idiot? I didn't think so when Caddy had a go at Sarah. You oughtn't to be so frightened of yourself.'

'I'm not,' he said, drawing a five-pointed star in spilt beer. 'The opposite.' He did not raise his eyes to her but made a triangle round the star—the boatyard pennant.

' "Once a king, always a king: once a knight is enough",' she read. 'I wonder where they get them, or do you think it's a cottage industry like reed-cutting? It *might* be interesting

115

what happens in the next few days, don't you think so? It's pretty much a case of liquorice all-sorts, a bag of. I don't know how struck Caradoc and our Tricia are but I can't entirely forget a certain incident in London.'

'He was probably drunk.'

'Why do you say that?'

'It was fairly apparent.'

After a moment she said: 'I can think of at least two other hypotheses.'

'They're ten a penny.'

'One—you're defending a fellow male. Two—you like to think of people tied up in couples, bundles of two. Without being rude, that might be a reaction to the split-up of your dad and Aunt Meg. No one on this trip's married for God's sake.'

'I don't know them.'

'Know *who*?'

'Roger and his girlfriend, Jack—you, come to that.'

'Sarah's Roger's sister. Now that *is* apparent.'

'My mistake.'

'We're nearly all brothers and sisters like a revivalist meeting.'

The beer talked, giggled and swore over mooring ropes. Away from the pub the darkness of the June night sizzled in the ears when given a chance. A whole bar-load was tripping every few yards. Boaty cries carried over the water.

Their boats lay further back from the general ruck, a select mooring chosen by the chance of man overboard. Leaving the lights of the other salooners they became once again themselves, but transformed from what they'd been at the boatyard, a voyage away.

'Those Shrikes are quite nifty.' Hubert's voice carried back from the semi-single-file imposed by a shouldering field which sweated scents as it grew.

'Hubert and Sarah.' William felt Janet's arm go round his waist. He placed one of his with careful *camaraderie* along

116

her shoulder. 'They might do each other good this week. How about that for a thesis?'

'How do you mean?'

' "Once a king, always a king ..." Sorry, Arthur—it was a joke. They seemed to get along together. It just struck me they might as well share all the hazards of the voyage. It's what I said in Wroxham: we've only got a few sailors and to stick Roger and Sarah together would be a waste, as well as boring for them.'

'They should sort that out themselves.'

'Mind you, it wouldn't be bad for them. It's time Hubert made his *debut*. Perhaps he already has—and, don't say it, it's not my business.'

'Your experiments again.' He was waiting for her arm to shift but it didn't.

'All right. That's what life is, isn't it? You try out things and if they fail you try something else.'

'People don't act like that.'

'Your mother did.'

It was his arm that was taken away and they stood between the field and the river whilst the others went on. A squall of laughter. Tricia's voice: 'I don't mind being raped, if I'm raped nicely.'

Silence rocked back. William stood, dangle-armed, aware of the tired little recurring situation. He was truly objective— that, if nothing else! The delayed shock of the afternoon was taken into account and all the other, older factors. There was her generosity, which he had come to accept—one possible baseline for some impossible graph.

'I shouldn't have said that. Sorry.'

'It doesn't matter.'

'Yes it does. Do I have to push you in the river? I would, if I hadn't had to fish you out once already. It does matter,' she sounded angry, 'what people do to each other.'

'I'm not saying *that* doesn't.'

'Well then,' she said in the dark. 'Of course all we really kick against is ourselves.' She walked on; he followed, various

117

things to say breaking the surface of his mind, but all as weak as water, none of them said.

Caradoc was half way up *Stella*'s mast, his heavy form stuck there. He was trying to sing 'The Good Ship Venus', sticking at the end of the second line and going back to the start. Suddenly he slid a foot or so. An appreciative audience filled the cockpit. 'How psychological!' Tricia was crowing. Jack, loosely embracing her bright red mac, was laughing enigmatically—or simply, as people laugh at chimpanzees. Roger and Sarah provided the other upturned faces, Roger crooning 'The Eton Boating Song' to the accompaniment of Sarah on saucepans.

Janet stepped lightly aboard. 'Where's my brother?' It was completely, intentionally out of key.

'I don't know, darling, where your brother is.' Apart from the timing of the words, Jack could have been completely sober.

'"I am not thy brother's keeper": Jesus H. Christ.'

'I wasn't asking you.'

'Temper,' said Tricia. 'Does she often lose it?'

'Janet? That would be telling. I think you left it in Denmark, didn't you, my sweet?'

'I was thinking of a meal, not a scene.'

'Can I help?' Sarah flourished her lid. 'I'm terrific with simple things like potatoes. You can't make spuds complicated; that's what I like about them, I think. Hubert's gone looking for fireflies. Can I help you, Janet?'

'It's mainly tinned beans.'

Double focus, he thought, stretched on the warm fore peak— Raymond Williams curling in the sun. Yes, like the visual reversal of a black and white pattern, like a child's chant with the words changing step as you said them. So that this flash of water was at once itself a three-dimensional ecosystem, a mass man had accidentally provided here in Norfolk on this one specific and amazing planet and also a lazy mirror of early summer and themselves. Compatible. Clear in his mind

118

the reed-stems at the mouth, sunlit to their watery roots, connecting—specific, ordinary, generating accidentally in him delight, which had stored too, evidently.

'Nice broad,' he said, cranking on one elbow to be friendly to hairy, reading Caradoc.

'The first broad is always the nicest. I had mine in the fourth form on top of an air-raid shelter. You went to Public School, didn't you?'

'Our headmaster attended conference. It was minor in every way.'

After a minute, Caradoc said: 'Jones Minor, I want you in every way.'

'I think the cold shower theory must have more or less worked at our place.'

'I sometimes hope I'll live long enough to enact all my fantasies.' Caradoc spoke almost wistfully. 'Then,' he added, 'I sometimes wish I'd never been born.'

'We must all do that sometimes.'

'Your sister doesn't.'

'Probably not. I hardly know her. We were divided by the divorce—that's a dozen years ago, when I went away to school. You must know all that.'

'First I've heard of it. We don't talk about the past on principle. Unless we're shopping for ideas. Then it's some classic period like L'Art Nouveau. Not classic? You watch out—the 'sixties are going to be like the good old 'nineties. Except *they* probably thought it meant something.'

'It did presumably—historically.'

'That's to assume history means something, which is more than I'd do.'

William sat up—planks which had been principally warm had become principally hard. Caradoc was a fool: working hypothesis. The likelihood of prolonged conversation with him had faded. Whoever had first had the idea of manning this fleet, it was a good idea. Such a quick catastrophe as yesterday's left the rest of the week open. He sat in general hopefulness like that of the reed stems, he too having dipped and risen. With subtly self-curbing deliberation he found his old OTC spectacles and snapped on their ear-twanging tentacles to sharpen the lessons out on the broad. On one boat Hubert and Janet harkening to Sarah, on the other his own sister fluttering happily between the two sailing men.

'There's that abbey!' It came up fast, dominated as in the brochures by ruined oasthouse or Norfolk windmill. His cry fell overboard. 'Close-hauled,' yelled Janet or something like that. He quite believed her: they were flying! His simple job was ballast, 'crew' was the polite word for it. Inches below the Bure dashed itself to pieces. Monastic windmill? He sketched a medieval praying machine. Leonardo's wastepaper bin. The wind bloweth where it listeth. Bloweth and we list. God, wanting prayer, had only to blow for it.

The other Shrike became close, bearing down at an even faster rate. Their own sail shivered as Janet threw the tiller and lost headway. Unable to picture the invisible forces, he knew impact was imminent. A shout of 'Fore!' preceded it. Jack's hissing prow came on, looking set for nothing but plain sailing. Lower than the swelping boom he got into the cockpit. The blow snapped the metal beading on their gunwale but, by pirouetting his craft, Jack had saved them from the worst. With a fusillade of canvas, they were on the other tack, the two of them, laughing like buccaneers.

'On purpose.' She wiped the sweat of her palms on her shorts leaving her hair to thrash over her face which was bolted up in anger. His 'I don't know' sounded like nothing. When she said nothing, he said, 'It could have been worse.'

'What are you talking about?'

'The accident.'

'Who said anything about an accident?'

'Incident then.'

'Calculated,' she said. 'No more and no less.'

'But if we hadn't stopped wouldn't they have gone astern?'

'What do you know about it?'

'Not much,' he admitted.

'You don't know Jack.'

'I said I didn't.'

'Well then.'

They bumped the bank. One of the laughing faces had been Tricia's. She might have suggested the incident—but Jack would not have acted on it?

'Now we're here,' she said, 'we may as well look at this ruin.'

The Shrike seen to, they walked across unusually springy turf. Half way there she caught his hand. Contact affected him objectively, allowing sensation to be intermediate, a means of observation. Touch implied a circuit diagram of her body and lit up the way round his. Subjectively it transformed the ruins, grass and sky. Close to, the abbey was even less like any idea of one. It was a human structure and that was all the meaning it had. Shapes were arbitrary and its dark red colour diametrically opposite to the grass. He missed her question, though she had let go of his hand.

'I said not a patch on Fountains.'

'You've been?'

'Yorkshire. Dark arcades, even a piscatory. I like my abbeys romantic.'

A ragged hole led into the great beehive. They were touched by the patchy light of the place, the queer cool of centuries. He said it must be a mill.

She shivered. 'Ugh, bats. Bats and monks give me the creeps. Cowled horrors. What are you doing?'

'Seeing if there are bats.'

'Why can't you take things on trust?'

Rubble faltered under his feet and a small landslide deposited him against her. He made a tottering embrace of it and for good measure landed a kiss on her chin. The smallest sound in her throat cleared him, but he was stuck ankle-deep in rubbish. 'Here.' Janet slipped her hand into his shirt and her tongue in his mouth. Her face moved back, looking at him. A tiny band of light on it, only the size of a highwayman's mask, sank into the irises. He was amazed at the changing subtlety of eyes. 'I suppose that was inevitable,' she said.

'I don't know.'

'Accidental?'

'You know, I slipped.'

'And God said: "I've heard that one before." ' She sneezed.

'Bless you.'

'I must be allergic. It's all right, not you—bats. I'll race you to the boat.'

Half way, he gave up—the golden apple the sight of her running ahead. He was speaking to himself for the first time since the worst attacks of the Sugdens. But 'All right' was what he was saying, 'all right'. And he was on equal terms with whatever there might have been to hear him.

'We were nosing through the bridge and we were rammed.' Hubert sank exhausted to the grass. 'She got us there on that cupful of wind, Sarah. We'd got half way through. Rammed. You'd never guess who.'

Janet said: 'Stay where you are, relax, take deep breaths. We'll come in. William won't mind.'

'I won't!' He tried a manoeuvre that was possibly impossible, levering the boat sideways with the quanting-pole. Someone had said, given a fixed point, he could move the Earth. The Shrike responded. Or else it was the magnetism of the bank, an established fact on this skinny, picturesque river. Sweat crawled around his scalp, festooned his back and chest. For a solid hour he had walked the great pole up and down whilst rich meadows simmered in a richer and richer light, increasingly like some painted Flemish landscape.

'Tom, Dick and Harry all on one boat. At the end of last term you'd not have expected to find them in the same sitting of Hall. It's fantastic.'

'I'm sure you're right, dear. It's called "coincidence".'

'I'd told them we were coming and apparently Harold's uncle owns a cruiser.'

'They couldn't bear not to be with you in the hols then—sorry, Vac.'

'You know what they can be like. Perhaps you don't. They immediately went into a barrage of remarks—you know, me and Sarah on the Shrike.'

'Brought maidenly blushes? Ignore me, love. I was going to say on Sarah's downy cheek.'

'Manghan can be choice.'

'She loved it, of course she did. *In flagrante delicto*'s okay, especially if it's a mistake. If they're so terrible, what are you doing abandoning her to them?'

'She sent me to say there's no point in going through the bridge. Moor here. We'll never get to the broad anyway, not tonight. Give us the mallet and I'll do you a round turn and two half hitches.'

'Did she teach you that as well?'

'Oh, belt up,' said Hubert.

'You must forgive us, mustn't she?' Manghan, transformed by suntan and toy peaked cap, did—or overdid—a few jive steps, his face upturned to the cabin ceiling and glazed by it. In him seemed the force of the summer night. 'We been done long voyage, ma'am.'

All afternoon William had felt his peripheral receptors doubled in power of gathering-in; all afternoon there had been only the simmering land, and Janet. But they had been in a mutual dance of holding off. In the cruiser of Harold's uncle there was scope for testing. What he had thought of as high spirits in Manghan wasn't that: behind the high cheek-bones, the intelligent, compressed smirk was pain he laughed at or suffering he juggled with.

'I'm hungry.' Harold tidied one of the bunks and slipped a sports coat from a hanger. 'That stew you concocted last night was disgusting.'

'Bloody good stew,' said Thorpe. 'Dick dug that beetroot fresh.'

'Dig that beetroot, man.'

'I suggest we find an eating-place.'

'You pay then.'

'If necessary, even that.'

'The Orton millions. Have you lot eaten?'

'I noticed there's a village dance on,' said Hubert. 'It's only an idea.'

'It's a great idea,' said Manghan. 'None of you'll have a hope if I'm there. I'm in the groove.'

'Is that what they call it?'

'It's a jolly good idea but I'll have to change. Won't you, Janet?'

'Behold the lily of the field in all its raiment is not attired like one of these.'

'The trouble is my things are all on *Stella*,' said Janet. 'Which is probably miles away.'

'You are about my size and Mummy packed me a trousseau.'

'All right—if you're sure you don't mind.'

'Short intermission,' said Orton.

'Of about one and a half hours.' Tom flopped dramatically on his berth. 'I have sisters.'

Manghan produced a contained explosion. 'You're always telling us. Why don't we ever see any? They can't be as bad as you. The women shortage back in the gilded madhouse and you don't even ask them to the May Ball. I'd have taken one of them for a small fee.'

'When they came up I was careful to keep them out of sight.'

'Big mates! There must be something wrong with them. Your nose. Or else they're so cock-tingling lush they're being kept for Dukes.'

'Kept for Dukes? The staple of your reading might as well be the weekly pap of women's magazines.'

'Let's go ashore.'

By now the dusk was drawing across. Other boats were making fast for the night. William wondered aloud about the *Stella*.

'That's a point,' said Hubert. 'With their engine they're probably in the broad but they must have guessed we'll never make it. Jack seems to know what he's at.'

'Yes. They might hang on there, expecting us. Officially, you can't cruise after nightfall.'

'Roger, Jack and your sister, isn't it? What happened to whatshisname?'

'Caradoc. I'm not sure. I think he went off yesterday.'

'In some sort of huff?'

'I don't know.'

'Remember I'm not getting at you in any way. Is it, you know, the scientist in you that makes you reluctant to guess?'

'Science *is* guesswork. That's not an answer either.' He was thinking of Janet, of all the years Hubert had known her, of her in him even. A hopeless lover already. Darkening water beginning to stir with the intimate lights of boats. Comfortably hopeless. 'I think he said it was business. It's hard to tell about other couples.' *Other* couples? 'I suppose because of my parents I'm reluctant to judge.'

'When your father went you were too little.'

'I remember things.'

The reflections washed stronger around them. Manghan and the others could be heard on their foray into the village.

'Perhaps you've been in the shadow of it.' Hubert spoke with his special straightness. 'Perhaps some people have to creep out of the shadow of a childhood. Alternative to the Wordsworthian patent shining light.'

The girls, plainly exquisite even at a dusky distance, hopped ashore.

'Fish and chips.'

They gathered on the bank. Tom, the practical one, issued portions. Harry apologised: 'Manghan had them soused with vinegar before we could stop him.'

'Prolefeed. Where I come from chips without vinegar would be like ... jugged hare without raspberry jam where you come from.' He went off into a private explosion at the water's edge.

'It wouldn't be so bad if there was any truth in it,' Orton said. 'You're painfully *petit-bourgeois* in fact.'

'The village seems a little small for a fried-fish shop.'
Sarah's upbringing told.

'It was a van,' said Tom Thorpe. 'Dick here hailed it. Young
Orton had two lots. Young Anstey was right about the dance,
it begins at nine.'

Manghan said: 'Young Manghan is going off the idea, Mr
Midshipman Thorpe.'

'When the ladies have changed?'

'You are charming but few.' Manghan bowed—Mephisto-
pheles with chip papers.

'Aren't we wasting drinking time?' Janet asked.

'Where the hell's he got to?'

'He wouldn't have taken a bike,' said Hubert. 'A tricycle
was too much for him to resist.'

'I don't know how he gets away with it.' Orton's pipe was
going great guns.

'He hasn't,' said Thorpe. 'What's the betting he crashes
into the police semi or runs over the vicar's cat?'

'He behaves,' continued Orton with a flare of insight, 'in
exactly the way he professes to despise.'

'You and your pipe,' said Janet. 'Don't be so dreary.'

'It was terribly funny though—a tricycle with drop handle-
bars. Whose do you think it is? Not the fat man's he had
words with. Wouldn't that be too ghastly?'

'It was funny at the time,' Hubert admitted.

'Wasn't it?' Sarah and Hubert laughed together.

'Come on, Arthur.'

'Where?'

'Anywhere. I want to say something.'

'All right.'

They turned from the lit pub yard and village street towards the darkness of the road. He tried to keep in step,
even changing his in the recommended Corps fashion—*one,
two*.

'What?' he asked at length, the length of old cottage gar-
126

dens bathed in new, nineteen-sixties lamplight. She said nothing.

In the sodium glare of lamps artfully bracketed to brick-work—producing new lurid dreams within?—she had been a figure in the neutralised wild apple-green and red of Sarah's dress; now she became differently unknown—less visible but less abstract.

'Or was it a ploy?' He felt the remark's drooping inapposite-ness—hopeless lover, hopeless remark. Anything he could say would topple. An owl cried.

She stopped, questioning.

'Owl.'

'Doing something awful with its food.'

'They regurgitate. The famous pellets. It puts them in a class of their own for research. You know, the evidence on a plate.'

'Ugh. Little things' skeletons.'

'Among other things. We had a man on owls.'

'I find it horrible,' she said. 'And I know it isn't. Coming to terms with the holiness of facts is something I'm not good at.' Another cry shook out. 'Ominous is right.'

'This man, I spent a night with him once in a hide. He could really get through to them. Imitate them.'

'Sometimes, now for instance, I imagine the world inside their heads, owls and animals. Strange! They select different things I suppose. Anyone can see the world in a grain of sand, but in an owl's head.... Brrrr.'

'Would you like my jacket?'

'With you in it?'

'I see.' He held her. They were in the middle of the road; he listened for cars. None, nor owls.

'Dick's a good dancer,' she said.

'Better than me.'

'Tons. But I thought we'd all get slung out. Did you feel superior—us superior lot of half-wits dropping in on Steeple Bumstead?'

'It's not a feeling I get much.' He shifted his stance, getting

127

a better—fortuitous—hold of her. But he felt like a tailor's dummy in a shop-window. Three checks to make him so—she, Jack, himself. Why isn't this apparatus working? One, two, three.

She laid her cheek on his lapel. That confused him. Calculated, not spontaneous, it might mean anything. Her hair was close and smelt like hair. A faint scent unfolding itself from Sarah's clothes, by association, suggested apple blossom. 'Now,' she said, 'you with all your equipoise won't be staggered at the next news which is that, failing the return of the good ship *Stella*, we shall have to kip on the Shrikes.'

'Yes.'

'Well, Hubert's quite willing to kip on Sarah's Shrike and Sarah ditto, if you see what I mean.'

'I see.'

'Which, Hubert thought, might make it embarrassing for us. Trust Hubert. That's why I went out with him for about an hour. If *Stella* returns of course ...'

'You're being careful so that I don't get the wrong end of the stick.'

'Am I? Which end is that?'

'I don't know, do I?'

'Let's get back to the Great Tricyclist Mystery.'

'Hardly any moon,' he said.

'Yes. The village looks like a place where people live.'

Behind their backs from the uncut cake of the Norfolk night an owl called, a kind of sonic cough. William remembered the owl man. He had got the owls to answer but never satisfactorily explained the gradations of meaning in their cries: a fresh pellet, a fresh death? Night revoked man's lease on all his measured fields. He felt himself catching Janet's fancies. The lights began to outline her walking figure. He caught her hand, enclosing its coolness; hers squeezed his. Everything was honed to question-marks.

They looked in the pub yard. 'It's back where it was.'

'Any sign of *them*?'

'Not a scrap. Go on to the boats.'

There they didn't need looking for—a party was in progress on the roof of the Orton launch.

He asked her the time.

'By my waterproof watch it's eleven.'

'*Stella*'s not here.'

'Surprise, surprise.'

'You'd imagine Jack would have got back, or got a message back somehow.'

'Would you? Let's join the revels.'

'Hi.' Sarah was semaphoring. 'We've found it's Tom here's birthday. He really didn't know. We were discussing horoscopes and he just said, "Good heavens, I'm twenty"—just like that, and he was. It must be super to find it's your birthday.' Hubert grabbed her knees, a necessary action. 'I'm quite canned,' she announced.

Harold found them places to sit and solemnly exhibited two bottles. 'I can recommend the Whitbread's.'

'Despite the evidence,' said Tom, 'and the fact I'm twenty ...'

'Many happy returns.' Janet said it straight, William noticed—his love noticed.

'Thanks. The general thesis was that a constant factor—I defer to your scientific presence ...'

William laughed. 'I don't mind being treated like Einstein.'

'Cheers. People have always been superstitious. It's a constant factor—it used to be religion that was the acceptably accepted thing and now it's science. But at any given time far more people were not putting their shoes on the table than were praying or checking the power-points.'

'They were wearing them,' said Janet.

'God, you women go in for this. Don't you see you have to wade through dubious statements to get a view of the target? Ranging shots.'

'It's all talk. The beautiful lady knows.' Manghan sat down, a little too hard, misjudging his landing. 'The only significance is in meaningful action, such as pedalling a tricycle.'

'I don't know what's significant in that,' said mellowed Orton.

'She could tell us.' Manghan's high-cheekboned face—which looked fixed, all mobility in eyes and mouth—stretched into an Idris lemon as he pulled it. 'The lady knows,' he said in gypsy tones.

'What Richard means is that action can be self-sufficient. It doesn't have to be part of something else. Riding a tricycle's no more pointless in itself than ... running with a bomb into an enemy dug-out. Don't you?'

'All that and more.' Manghan glugged beer.

'Existentialism?' Tom put in a word.

'Ex-ist-entialism. I exist therefore I think. That's cool, man: I like that. Have some more *booze*. I want everyone to stop doing what they're always doing and do something else. Instead of shaving every day, cut up the morning paper, instead of ...'

'Going to the lavatory?'

'That's a point. Tie a knot in it.'

'Don't give up now,' said Harold with more Whitbread's. 'This is "I dreamed of a new Heaven and a new Earth".'

'Shag off.'

'In the words of the poet.'

Manghan responded with his George Formby imitation done at first to groans; but his *Leaning on a Lamp-post* was so good that the applause was perfunctory only in irony. And he stood laughing at himself on the cabin roof, the first slip of the new moon balanced on his head.

'Dunlopillo time.' Janet got up. 'Brother and Sister Sarah have disappeared.'

'That's not you going already?' Harold was there to carry out the last rites of hospitality, even to handing Janet down the gangplank. Tom, who had passed into the silence before the storm, flapped a pallid hand. Manghan, tuning up for Harry Lauder, bowed from above.

'Mind the ropes.' She took his hand. 'It's a wonder the neighbours don't complain.'

'Listen.'

'What?'

'Nothing. I thought I heard an engine.'

'They'll be bedded down by now—one way or another.'

'Perhaps it was Dick's bagpipes.'

'Desperate Dick,' she said.

'Yes. He is somehow.'

'This is theirs. Ours is further along.'

'You're sure Sarah isn't expecting you?'

'What? She isn't.'

Aboard, Janet lit the Calor gas. Everything was noticeably shipshape.

'Cocoa or Nescafé? Your sister seems to keep everything in its place.'

'She does.'

When the watched kettle boiled Janet said: 'It's a bit like your Sugdens.'

Of all the things he could have said, he said: 'Fewer suicides.'

'You'd need to be a pinhead to get in this oven. Pinheads don't kill themselves.'

'Lemmings do wholesale. What's called a "population crash" in the trade.'

'I'd forgotten them. Yes, it upset me for days. Hours. Do they really think they'll cross the Atlantic?'

'No one knows.'

'A new life over the horizon. That's not very original of them.'

'Some stay put.'

'But next year it's their turn.'

'Unless the clever and nasty ones always send the others.'

'That's the most unscientific thing you've ever said.'

'I wish you'd all drop my scientific reputation, especially you.'

'Sorry.' Janet sat rather cautiously on one of the berths. Cocoa steam tangled with her hair.

He wondered if she had decided it was for him to act. She

131

had praised action, agreeing with Manghan. But then she had invoked the Sugdens: equally a cousinly mateyness might be all, the kiss at lunchtime a flukey nothing. He looked quickly up from where the skirt of Sarah's dress had rucked. In her hands the cocoa wreathed her face and sentiment could cusp about her face.

'Sarah and Hubert,' he said, shaking his head—a phoney.

'I think Sarah wants to get rid of her "reputation" and sees Hubert as a nice way of doing it. I think she's using him, but it might do him good as well.'

William nodded, reminded of an occasion when Corbett confided some theory way beyond him and he had been forced to reciprocate the familiarity with nods and wise looks.

'Of course,' said Janet, 'I said "do him good" forgetting that those two are some sort of heirs to the third largest merchant bank. From what she's told me her upbringing was about 1910. You know, my father used to substitute "mummy" and "daddy" for "nanny" in *Now We Are Six*. I mean I bet her nanny didn't.'

'I like Hubert.'

'I like him. Then I wonder if he's naive or innocent. Or just good. But is anyone good? And I sort of cluck and wonder if it'll survive in him. I don't worry about John, say, at all—jets notwithstanding. I'm running a campaign for words like that. I actually used "albeit" last week and something else. I think it was "contradistinction".'

'Do you want to "use the bathroom"?'

'There you are. Pure Sugdens. Have you *been* on these? They flush. Still, it's better than the chemical horror.'

'I'll water the stars.'

'You don't have to.'

'I can check the ropes.'

'Look.' She stuck out her wrist. 'Midnight.'

When the person who was neither Jack nor Hubert but a man taking his dog for a walk had passed, William let out the Whitbread's. For an instant relief was blinding. Unburdening a full bladder, unburdening a full heart. Bladders fuller

132

oftener. Plot as a graph. That poem of Manghan's 'When lives were played like instruments not cards'—listened for bagpipes —he'd written because he was playing his hand reckless. Yes, Manghan, self-elected joker of the pack. And clowns and broken hearts and final spurts of transmogrified Whitbread's. That would have filled more pints than he'd drunk, even allowing for the cocoa. Body added interest, leaching out its wastes, dumbly, dutifully. But staking its claim too. Stargazing settles Fate.

She'd had time to be in bed, blanketed to her hair, a hummock just awake enough to say goodnight. Jack as nebulous as nebulae reared above, too huge to be substantial.

He remembered to check the moorings. Hubert's half-hitches were in order, albeit done hastily and notwithstanding men trailing dogs.

She was combing her hair. 'Hullo. Other people's combs are all right but other people's toothbrushes are immoral. What with Sarah's clothes as well, I'm a proper parasite.' She undressed quickly, without self-consciousness. She said, 'Gay Paree,' when she got the suspender-belt off, a thing tagged with black lace. 'I hope she's a bit thinner round the middle.' Then she got into the bunk, pants and brassiere retained. Miserably he felt put out of his misery and took his shoes off. She was watching him, again quite openly.

'Quite a few stars out there,' he said.

'Trillions,' she said brightly.

He turned his pillow—last known resting place of hairy Caradoc—and a small box hopped onto the floor between them.

'Fancy keeping those under the pillow.'

'Yes.'

'Do you want to come in with me?'

'You know that. Are these comb or toothbrush?'

'Neither, I *hope*. "Did you imagine it like this?"'

'I don't think I saw it ever happening.'

'Don't talk.'

'What I can't understand. I can't understand about Jack.'

133

He spoke from the safety of his shirt.

'Don't talk. Can anyone understand anything? I'm giving up trying to.'

'Can't. Curiosity's a brain function.'

'It's what killed the cat.'

'Tenth time round.'

'I like your chest. It looks honest.' She laughed. 'I just said that but it does. Go on, tell me why gorillas bang them.'

When he had found his way back in the dark (a notice near the switch: 'Conserve your battery'), he felt for the bunk and she reached out, catching his knee. 'Thought that was your elbow.' When his hand landed on her breast it was puzzled, expecting cloth there. Sorted out, they lay close, his arm round her shoulders gingerly gentle. Inches from their faces water licked and sucked the hull. 'I can't promise to be any good at this.'

'Relax, this is a friendly.'

Time stretched, Time stopped.

'There.' Kindness had been. They lay in the same lock. He rescued the blanket. She came back with a kiss in his ear. Plog. The Shrike lulled like the first of all rocking, cradled in water. Existence flapped, unthinkable. This had been a cleat for it. She slithered over him, flesh back on its own terms.

BOOK THREE

ONE

Blinking in the traffic, Janet saw again the house half ominous in its agedness, marooned in Cheshire meadows. It had been as galleon-like as the calendar showed. But shut—perhaps as well with this lot, leaving only the moat to avoid which she had, just; and not Ming vases, tottery suits of armour, whatever was within. Backseat so quiet, she looked in the mirror. Unbelievable harmony. Houses as means of transport made theirs a couchette. Mid Twentieth-Century express (wasn't there one in the States?) zooming through the kids' childhood into her own middle-age, the next stop. The rural trafficlights changed and she had lost the engine.

Yes, the disasters had all been minor and there was no trouble killing time with children: they killed it for you. Two hours at the place and at this rate one hour to get back, meaning practically no time for bedtime, baby-sitting, buzzing off. 'Rupert,' she said, voice on tape, 'must you?'

'I'm not.'

'Don't then.'

Good and truly stuck on this hill.

'Say thankyou to Mrs Goodyear.'

'Mark's tired,' she said. 'He's been very good.' If very good encompassed pushing Alice's iced lolly down her throat.

'I didn't know what to do with myself,' said Sheila.

'I know.'

'All that lovely free time. I rang Robert but he'd gone to Chester. I don't suppose you've the time for a cup of?'

'I really haven't.'

'That's right. The party, isn't it? Lucky Janet.'

'I don't know about that.'

'Wow, without a husband!' Sheila fluttered eyelids intricate as Cellini—what she had been doing perhaps with her afternoon—allure with the stops out for no one in particular or for Robert who had gone to Chester. She stood on the tiptoe of further speech, one of her indigenous, her unassumed mannerisms. All she said was: 'Say bye-bye to Rupert, Mark.'

'Bye, poo-bottom.'

They exchanged routine horrors; Janet took hers off through the gap in the 'ranch-style' fencing.

By expensive oversight the immersion had stayed on. With Rupert and Alice down in record time she had the water if not the leisure for a bath. In went the Badedas, present from mother-in-law promising lean saviours in old Rolls-Royces. Gold, Badedas and myrrh. Since fantasy had gone public she had given it up, she prided herself. What a day, every day! Heat or the additive produced uncommon steam but, instead of colour-litho promises she saw a mirrorful of little boys animated about the *Magic Roundabout*, for all the world like theatre critics with the varnish stripped off—their little boys' energies gaily gobbling up the world. She'd smiled at the time and not noticed. Then Sheila encapsulating all that was hopeless about the estate, that is by judging against ideas—alternatively you judged people by what you knew of yourself. Censure or charity, or a mixture of both. She got the plug out with her toes, a habit of years, and herself out before second thoughts set in. The wiped steam gave a glimpse that was a pleasant surprise. The doorbell chased her.

'They shouldn't wake up. Gladys, isn't it?'

'Glenys.'

'Sorry, it's such a rush. Do you want to look at them?'

'No. It's alright.'

'I just will then.' Rupert flat out as usual and surrounded by all he possessed in some order of its own and the baby

138

ruminant with dummy. Some tucking in. Glance for sharp toys and see their sleeping faces irradiate a path.

'They seem O.K.' She hunted out her boots from beneath the settee, zipping them under the sceptical gaze of Glenys's boyfriend, a fountain of hair and medallions. He said: 'Where's the box?'

'Sorry?'

'Television.' Five syllables.

'We haven't one.'

'Old-fashioned liberals,' he seemed to say. She laughed apologetically, unnecessarily for he appeared to have lost interest.

'Let me show you the fridge. There's eggs and things and instant coffee. Or beans, if you can work that thing. All right?'

'Super,' said Glenys and Janet left the house with some hope that the children might survive. Fussing with car keys, she fetched a sigh and was for a moment full of high tension, standing on the driveway like some electric pylon without wires. Or else it was static from the car handle. Reaction perhaps to the rush. To the boyfriend.

Sheila had drifted out to wish her a good time. Curiosity or Sheila's attempt at neighbourliness. She shrugged it off, whipped on a smile.

Turning into the main road, ought she to have asked Sheila to keep an eye on the baby-sitters?

'It was built by a cotton millionaire.' Tony Garret pointed out some gothic lettering above the hall fireplace.

' "Home, Sweet Home," ' she read.

'Good, isn't it? Everything else some arty Johnny from London must have done.'

'I still don't really know whose it is.'

'It belongs to Carole. That's the remarkable thing, she's an assistant lecturer in our department. But with all this to go home to who needs salary?'

'I suppose not.'

'Old Bill's up at Fell Head again, is he? Internationally Biologising. Carole's hot on peat flora—the air at coffee-break used to be thick with it. Oh, I was saying you're pretty hot on peat flora and here you are.'

'I was admiring the fireplace.'

'You're Janet Goodyear, right? Pleased to meet you. That's nothing, you should see the closet.'

'She means the cloakroom,' said Tony. 'It's her semi-American ancestry.'

'If I didn't know this guy ... but, Janet, you're still with your coat.'

'Come through here, isn't it swish?' The girl with red hair opened a way outside. 'These café tables, wherever did she get them? I've only seen these umbrella things in Paris.'

'Not to mention the lights.'

'They're from the Christmas tree in Albert Square. Carole's like that—she gets things done.'

'Her step-father happens to be an alderman.' A boy came out of the shadows. 'You like whisky? This bottle's got her old man's name on it: personalised.'

'It's not Christmas. They may as well be used as stashed away.'

'Abused, bird. They're city property.' He took a fiery swig.

Janet said: 'Come to that, it's not your whisky.'

'You don't say so? But don't get me wrong—I don't want to bug you girls, why should I? I don't know you. I don't know your credentials. How about we sit at one of these dicky tables and have a chat. Like Paris in the hairy old twenties. Glasses and everything.' He disappeared.

'Is he drunk?'

'I shouldn't think so.'

'Who was in Paris in the 'twenties?'

'Well,' said Janet, 'Ezra Pound probably and that lot. Expatriate Americans,' as it came back to her. 'Paris in the 'twenties, Berlin in the 'thirties, nowhere in the 'forties, New

140

York in the 'fifties and London in the 'sixties.'

'And now Altrincham in the 'seventies.'

'Anywhere in the 'seventies.'

'Here—three glasses. We'll depersonalise the rye.'

'Without a qualm.'

'Right. Representing the masses, we'll appropriate it.'

'The holy masses.' The red girl giggled.

'I'm serious. Don't wag the Pope at me.'

'From what you said about the fairy lights though, your attitude surprises me,' said Janet.

'My "attitude" is political. You know the old one about exploiting the system to bleed it white, dossing down on someone's floor and charging Hilton expenses?'

'It's a new one on me,' said Janet.

'Everything is a political act.'

'That *sounds* all right. What you say sounds like moral doublethink to me.'

'I'm single-minded.'

'I must be simple-minded then.'

'You said it. Cheers. The way it is now you have to stand up and be counted.'

'What, when I've just sat down?' said red-head.

'Playing with words is like playing with drugs: it doesn't get anywhere. Truth is situational.'

'Is that what it is?' Janet swilled her whisky round the glass, crock of gold tinkling with the fairy rainbow. Truth buried at the end of every rainbow.

'I suppose you vote Labour?' he asked.

'I don't see how you get to that but it has been known, yes.'

'And teach university?'

'Not even at it. Sorry.' Here he was triumphantly categorising but not hostile—like a doctor running ahead on diagnosis and about to break triumphantly into prognosis, like Sherlock Holmes coming out with 'I think you spent your youth in Singapore and have a left-handed grandmother', only to be told 'No.' Equally it was hard for her to make sense of him. Being older than he was put her at a disadvantage. Or she could see herself coming to think that. And guilt by association—William taught university, that is when he wasn't up at Fell Head investigating peat.

'Parties are happenings. Precisely analogous to any other art-form. Orgies are literally decadent in proportion to the falling-off of structure.'

'Parties don't just happen, believe me. Janet, where have you been? Meet Erich Southey who's a real networked art critic.'

'Delighted.' He wrinkled his nose to hitch gold-rimmed glasses.

'He saw *Satyricon* as a late-night movie and I think he's a teeny bit disappointed by this little bean feast.'

'I said nothing of the sort.' He stage-managed a little tripping laugh. 'I'm purely a viewer of the scene.'

'Aren't you part of it?' put in Janet.

'Do you mean my tie? I'm afraid now it's what we do in Manchester today they did in London yesterday.' He peered at the label. 'Not being M & S is all that can be said for it.'

'It's ages since I was even at a party. It must be ten years.'

'I don't believe you.' Tony Garret swung a tray of sliding snacks through a gap in the crowd. 'As one spaceman said to another spaceman, "I'm worried by the lack of gravity of the situation."'

She laughed more than the remark justified.

'What are you drinking?'

'Liquorish all-sorts. I'm randomly sampling.'

He looked at her. 'Take it easy though.'

'Oh, I am.'

'Just let me get shot of this grub.'

''Bye.'

'Who are you?'

'Economist.'

'Really?' Janet rather carefully nodded. 'Common Market.'

'There you are, Janet. Where've you been? Al here's flying out to advise on manpower-planning. How about that?'

A plane went over, douching them with noise.

'Where's he going? Where are you going, Al?'

'The Virgin Islands.'

'I see.'

Carole exploded. 'Gee, you never said that. You never *said* that. Manpower planning in the Virgin Islands! That takes some beating.'

'Holding aside all the connotations,' (however had she managed that?) 'what do they do in the Virgin Islands?'

'Subsist,' said the affable economist. 'You know how these places are—one primary product: cocoa probably, or coffee. I'd better find that out and then hotels, tourists in Bermuda shorts.'

'Al, have you got Bermuda shorts? I'd give a hundred dollars to see you in those Bermuda shorts.'

'As a governmental guest—or is it High Commission?— I shall take good care to pack a dinner-jacket.'

'They're probably exploited?' Janet asked.

'Probably, probably. Exploitation is what economics is all about. When I get there I'll do the algebra for them.'

'And have a ball,' said Carole.

'I dare say they'll show a proper appreciation of my abilities.'

'The really cool thing about this shot was that it played everywhere except their faces, but everywhere.'

'Letter from him in the *T.L.S.*—short but incomprehensible.'

Random sampling. What was it William did? Shut his eyes and threw the thing he dug soil with anywhere, then somewhere else—and so got results mathematically true throughout.

Down, she looked on the fiesta of *Pernod* umbrellas, Christmas lights, a fountain behind the azaleas which must have been only just turned on and dark heads and fair heads and one or two bald heads—people strange from above; up, the moon almost fully floodlit through eaves larded with quirky woodwork. Her small room was under the eaves, taking the warmth of the sky or else saving up the afternoon sunshine like those moonbugs on Rupert's tea-cards.

Janet walked about the room. It was unfurnished but clean and carpeted. She walked back to the window, looked down, looked up. In her head she was inside such a room, climbed to on whisky, gin, Beaune—oh, and a Pernod, as advertised. *Parapluies.* Never the mistress of French, though it had featured in her London General. Parasols—but that had been Englished, flattened. They were neither in fact. It was one of William's tricks or gifts to see facts in front of him, things as they were. A bit had rubbed off if only for such purposeless thoughts as she had.

Paranuits, paralunes. And back to tea-cards.

Holding her own arms along, she saw herself again in the mirror. She hadn't Sheila's obsession with flesh but here she could comfort herself a little, make love to herself a little.

Whoever it was entered in such silence that she might have jumped in turning hadn't she felt the presence, spying it from the top attic of her mind. William—as seen when at odds with him—would have explained it in terms of air pressures. In the doorway it was Carole.

'It's sure hot in here.'

'Under the roof.'

'I get over the roof at these gigs. This place's for a breather. What do you think of it, the party?'

'It's just right. The lights and the parasols.'

'Yeah?'

'It must have taken some arranging.'

'Telephone, that's all. You can hire the stuff and they come right along and fix it. The fountain? It's only dollars, Janet honey. With dollars "she shall have music wherever she goes". Say, I also hired musicians and they don't show up.' Carole opened the windows to the full and leaned dangerously

144

forward. 'Guess what, I can see the States.'

'On a good day the Town Hall clock, you might.'

'No, come and see.'

Janet realised she meant the moon which had backed further behind the finical eaves. She also craned forward to look at it.

'You can kinda see Mailer striking matches.'

'Striking metaphors,' said Janet, rather thoughtlessly.

'Right!' Carole saw wit she didn't. 'Speaking as an ecologist, I rather we hadn't loused up that little old ball, but as the all-American American, part of me reaches out to it. As a woman for Christ's sake, literally. Now we even menstruate to the Flag.'

'I still find it hard to believe.'

'Any harder than anything else? We're all in orbit.' Carole's arms slipped round her. They were still leaning out, riskily perched above the party; first Janet thought she was being pushed then, almost simultaneously, that Carole was saving her from falling. Carole's hand slipped down her side and on to her thigh, then up, then down from her breast to her belly where it moved in deft massage for a moment or two.

They were in the room, apart.

'I wanted to do that.' Carole dug cigarettes out of a tasselled pocket in her tasselled jerkin. 'I guess you don't do that to your guests. It's more being American than anything else. More Long Island I mean than Lesbos Island. Say it, honey, whatever it is, say it.'

'I'm puzzled I suppose. A bit. I'm not shocked.'

'That's the alcohol, dear. Relaxes you. It's tough being from the States, like being a spoilt kid is tough. You know? That was stupid of me to feel you like that. It was stupid. I'd like to know you, to be your friend—I would really. Then I go and do that. Sorry—do you smoke? These are from the other side—they carry the warning.'

'I'll have one now.'

'Sure. Let me light it.'

Carole's lighter lit the cigarette and their faces intimately.

145

'You're shaky,' said Carole. 'My God, you must think I'm a real Sapphist.'

'No, I don't. It's all day with the children and Bill being away. You see? Corny. He helps a lot. He's good with them in some ways I'm not.'

'But when he goes off it's you who's lumbered.'

'I don't mind that. They are wearing. But they're—innocent.'

'Motherhood. I really do admire that. But you oughta meet mine. The way she played that role! It was sickly. I don't mean sick—sickly. Do you know she invented little tête-à-têtes that were meant to have happened between us? Little confidences I'd never have given the bitch got dragged out when she was showing me off, her little kid in a dandy dress. There I go. Being me is a disease. Why not let's get back to the party?'

'When you're in it—motherhood—it's not so much a state of being as a situation you're in. If that's a distinction.'

'You go on being you.'

'Yes! And wondering what that is.'

'It's in the air, baby—don't tell me it isn't.'

Occasionally, as now, Janet doubted the premises of her existence. So why was she here rather than elsewhere and why *should* Time have such a gripping and unchallenged hold?

Here was at one of the little tables. The musicians, just three of them, had appeared and run through their repertoire and nobody was asking for more. Off they bundled to the next booking. 'Four in one night, folks. Is this a record?' They had been too innocuous to provoke any hostility. Long cables snaking through flowerbeds connected them with their van. It was like a fairground generator but the noise they produced had no vulgarity. At home with Leonard Cohen, the Beatles, Ewan MacColl—accomplished and bogus, they held their audience with technology and treated them to bland harmlessness. They were almost as good as a record-player and they were called *The Nuclear Fissionaries*.

146

She had the winebottle by the scruff of its neck, not that drought threatened, not that she cared much for drinking, usually. The label had a particularly pleasant picture on it— a village in a flat landscape with small but detailed figures. The wine was dark red and full-bodied. She had shown off the label during a Leonard Cohen and had commended full-bodiedness to the art critic—or the economist, being smiled at but not heard.

The wine had done things to time and place: all things were acceptable, no longer hustling down a channel but raining their own rhythms on a wide and widening drum. Tipsy, if not drunk. Tipsy, yes. Drunk, no. Was tipsy a synonym though, or a measure of degree? Kind or degree? Kind of. Squiffy, plastered, blotto. Old slang hanging like gardening trilbies in the hall at home. Inebriated was William's word, her husband's sort of word. Accurate. Facts, when you came down to them, had the edge.

In the post-Nuclear silence conversations had started again.

'Marx.'

'I should even hesitate to call Marx an economist quite frankly.'

'I don't care what you call him.'

'I grant you he's interesting as a typical nineteenth-century thinker.'

'Your interest, no listen, your interest is disinfectant. "Interesting" must be the most dismissive word in your vocabulary.'

'I don't quite follow the point you seem to be trying to make.'

'I'm stating facts, brother.'

Janet found she had intervened, rising from her chair and interposing herself between the two conversationalists. She seemed to hold them and all they were saying in a crystal ball of understanding.

'Let me introduce. Al, an economist who is going to the Lesbos Islands. Oh, a friend of earlier who thinks truth is situational. There. That's what I think as well, I think. And

147

facts—I like those. There's something inviolate about facts. In fact they've got a bad name they don't deserve. I mean Truth of course. "Beauty is Truth, Truth Beauty; that is all ye know on Earth and all ye need to know."'

'You again.'

'That's right.'

'If you don't mind, I was explaining to this *academic* the facts about so-called Western Civilisation. It's based on manipulation by the powers-that-be of the media, the institutions and the family unit. The academic freedom and freedom of speech you're so fond of don't *need* to be attacked; they cloak the Conspiracy without.'

'Which conspiracy is this?'

'There's only one.' The whisky-appropriator sighed, an expression of patience. 'Capital, Parliament, so-called Democracy.'

'Three.' Janet felt protective towards her vision of truth which had not had justice done to it. 'That's three things.'

'Three-in-one,' said the economist. 'Now we're dealing with a mystic.'

'You make me sick, know that? You make me puke,' said the mystic.

'Mutual. Except my stomach is stronger I expect.'

'Look,' said Janet, 'I thought we were talking about truth, weren't we?'

'With him?' The economist snorted into his glass.

'What do you know about it?'

'Me?'

'You, quoting bloody Tennyson. You might be all right for a night, sister, but argument's not your strong point.'

'That's pretty insulting.' Al took off his jacket. She wondered if it was especially warm, it was growing late. 'I'm going to punch your nose.'

'Wait a minute.' She saw facts taking a jump ahead, or sideways. This wasn't going to happen. 'It's idiotic.'

'I couldn't do anything. I couldn't think.'

148

'Not expecting it.'

'I wasn't.' She thought how remarkably unexpected things were. After more than thirty years the expected never quite happened. She said nothing however. The thought was comfortable. Tony's old car was large, comfortable and safe. All tension was being shed in the dissection of past crisis. 'Being squiffy didn't help, mind.'

Tony Garret laughed. 'He up-overed the table and that cove from Economics hit someone's head.'

'That made it worse. He was being chivalrous, if you'd believe it.'

'I would actually.' Tony negotiated the Parkway—trees in their first flush of foliage sculpted by its soaring lights. In his warm car she slept.

And was gently shaken out of sleep. 'Seemed a pity to wake you.'

'God, what time is it?' Not exactly a headache, something bisected her brain, a globe twisted at the equator, severing continents. 'Those baby-sitters!'

'We took them home.' He sounded, quite rightly, pleased with himself.

'I owe them money.'

'They settled for one twenty.'

'That's fantastic. Weren't they mad?'

'They weren't anything definite.'

'Didn't Rupert wake up?'

'Not a peep apparently.'

'I've been quite hopeless. Come in. Are we back?'

'Number twelve.'

'You'll have a coffee. What did I do with the car?'

'I didn't let you do anything with it.'

'I wasn't trying to drive?'

'You were trying to get in.'

'Was I? Hullo, I've got my coat on. Shh, don't wake the monsters.'

'Let me.' She stood back and he opened the door, finding the right key quicker than she did in daylight. In the kitchen

149

the tube shot summer lightning before going on. He said it was the starter.

'I didn't know that. Excuse the washing-up. That's funny.' Five opened tins marched along the draining-board, each stuffed with wrapping paper, peelings, egg shells. 'They've eaten everything in the house. I said something about eggs. Macaroni, prunes, Swedish meatballs—what could you make with all that?'

'Indigestion. They must have had an orgy.'

'They were the things we never ate. Have you ever had tinned Swedish meatballs?'

'Did they break this?'

'The Cona! I never liked that.'

'You're taking it all remarkably well,' said Tony.

'Better see the kids are all right.' Janet went up and opened their door: they were. In the bathroom she caught sight of herself and with some finger-combing looked better than she felt. Tony Garret was grinding coffee beans when she got down.

'You should have let me do that.'

He held up the cat's plate in halves. 'Probably just clumsy. Your kids were in one piece?'

'It's a good thing they didn't wake.'

The kettle came to the boil. Tony looked round the bright room. His face was tired but alert with interest; he seemed at ease and she felt quite at ease with him. 'Machine for living in,' she said, then—cleverer still: 'Infinite hire-purchase in a little room.'

'You ought to see where I live off Cambridge Road. They must be saving it for some outdoor museum project—you know, the genuine bit of Mancunian slum.'

'I ought to thank you, honestly. I must be out of practice at going out by myself. Come into the sitting-room and sit down.'

'You hadn't met Carole before?'

'Around the university I might once.'

'She's unusual for a botanist.'

'Speaking as a botanist.'

150

'Me? I'm dead normal.'

'Glad to hear it.'

'I'd botanise on my mother's grave. In fact that would be difficult as she was cremated.'

'I can't tell a bergamot from a sea-anemone but I like plants. Do you like that? Ordinary cow parsley, isn't it? All green and white.'

'Like your dress.'

'That's grey and white.'

'Visually. Like the florescence. Airy.'

'I hadn't thought of it as airy.' She squinted down at the print which did enclose space similarly to the branching stems.

'Nice dress,' he said.

'Lewises.' She laughed. 'Sorry, I spend most of my time talking to Sheila next door. Housewife's choice—Hobson's choice. "Have a biscuit, there's a special offer."'

'Is there?'

'I mean it's the sort of thing we say.' She took off one boot, pushing it beneath the settee—coincidentally where it had come from some hours before. The zip on the other seemed to jam. He moved next to her. 'You'll snag those tights.' Neatly his fingers made it run free.

'You're very good at things.'

'Quite good. It's mainly a matter of concentration.'

'I'm usually thinking of half a dozen things at once.'

'Such as?'

'I don't know.'

He held her loosely and had undone the back of her dress. Her breasts were expecting his touch. His hand managed the fastening of the brassiere and now his fingers moved in, remaining still where Carole's had hastily been.

'I don't know if this is a good idea.'

'It isn't an idea.'

'You ought to stop.'

'Yes.' Now—and again he had done it without effort and without her compliance—above the waist she had no cover-

151

ing but his arm. His head was forward, lips on her clavicle; her eyes on the familiar lightshade tinily rigged with dust.

'It's late,' she said.

Tony's face rose inches from hers and smiled. It was a perfectly disarming smile. She did not want to be disarmed.

'They say "better late than never".'

'They say all sorts of things,' she said, which sounded arch.

'If I stay I could take you back in the morning for your car.'

'Yes ... or I could catch a bus.'

'You could catch a bus.'

'Just now I'm catching a cold.'

'Which is a good reason for going somewhere warm, like a bed.'

'That's one reason.'

'I know another.'

'You're amazing,' she said. 'Do you often do this?'

He returned to nuzzling her shoulder and said slowly: 'No. It seems to have happened this time.'

'The settee's quite comfortable.'

He moved adroitly to lower her but something as unchosen as the former expectancy of breasts stiffened her back.

'What?'

'I meant for you to sleep on.'

'Make your mind up, Janet.'

'I seem to,' she said.

'I'm not that much of a sod. I don't see why we can't simply go ahead. It's love as well. We both want to. Why do you have to bring guilt into it? The settee's fine. Why not?'

'Or, equally, why.'

'Because I know it would be good. Good itself, good for us. I mean it. And you do, so why make me talk about it? Bloody hell, I'm alive—I respond to stimuli.'

'I think I'd better cover them up.'

'Christ, don't do that. Okay, here's your bra.'

'Good boy.'

152

'You've had a narrow escape,' he said, casting around to find bitterness.

'You don't need to tell me.'

'I'll stay on my settee *and* drive you in my bloody car then ... if you're sure.'

'It's because I'm not sure.'

Her last line, her exit. How tailored to let herself off gracefully and leave him ruefully self-congratulatory, but off the peg in fact. A turn up for the books at some a.m. She turned over and looked gummily at the alarm. It said nothing, no tick-tock—stopped! Dead, never to start again. Suddenly she brushed round the other side of the bed—no one there, neither small nor big. Janet sat up, convinced it was eight-o'clock. Her town-dwelling ears were attuned to traffic background and its tell-time decibels. Her children must be dead! Tony may have scorched off to his slum.

But she fed the lot of them—wide-eyed Alice shamed into something like table manners and saying in her voice of doom 'Man, mummy'; and Rupert pretending to know about football. 'The Irish got two goals and United got a post. When I'm seven my daddy's going to get me real football boots.'

TWO

He awoke to rain in the early light, gallons of it, thousands of tons falling as far as the ear could hear, past gutters and walls where it clucked companionably to a further sound on the near paddock; and beyond that the ear imagined grid upon grid, sound behind sound—measurement, a partial seizing of the great coruscating mass lying over the high fells.

Only Bellsize's beard was visible, projecting almost vertical like a red hedge. William carefully propped his own head. It was characteristic of Bellsize to sleep with his beard thrust out. Only he was not asleep.

'Morning,' said Bellsize.

'Only just. I make it six.'

'I always get up at six.' Bellsize laughed. 'Bloody lie. I always mean to get up at six. Bloody human beings, they sit up all hours ruining their eyesight and then lie in bed like hogs as long as they can. I include myself.'

'It must have been raining all night.'

'A good soak. I like that: all that peat guzzling up the stuff. I can see us in a few years' time forced up here by population pressure. I'm assuming a crash of some kind. A few ecologists and hill farmers up here in the rain. I work in Birmingham—ever been? When I wake up in the morning do you know what really gets me?'

'No.'

'It's not the atmospheric poisons and it's not overpopulation, though I've got four kids, God blast me, and they're usually somewhere, everywhere, the little buggers, up my armpits, kicking me in the crotch, plucking my beard.'

William converted something in his throat into a cough.

154

'Could be any number of things,' he said weakly.

'You're dead right. It's frogs. There's not a frog within ten miles of where I put my head, except in the tanks and you know what that's like, you can't keep frogs. Not one free honest-to-God frog. That's terrible.'

'I agree.'

'May as well get up. I'm off this morning and I need a couple of dozen to take with me. I always leave it till the last minute. Only fair on them. My wife Jean can't understand why I talk in the morning. I'll get up now and have a good shit and get out into the field. I've been trying this business of chewing twigs to clean my teeth. Saw it done in Malaya last year.'

'What's it like?'

Bellsize was quiet long enough to suggest a relapse into sleep and William was himself beginning the long swim down.

Bellsize cackled. 'Horrible.'

Fell Head was staffed on the domestic side by the Coulthards. He farmed the few fields around the station with their special tagged sheep and kept the three-mile track from falling into the torrential beck. He would rescue snowfast Land-Rovers with his Ministry tractor and smile from a distance, but he kept himself to himself. She, with a minimum of talk, terrorised most visiting scientific workers. A small woman the colour of bog oak, she subverted normal standards of judgement and did it without recourse to landladylike ways. Her unspoken view of things powerfully prevailed as in the matter of breakfast, especially then. It was served on the dot of eight by being put 'on t'side' which was an Aga. Either on a shrivelling hot-plate or cold iron in a draught, by two minutes past bacon or porridge had gone to extremes. It was as if breakfast was not something she held with: it was a concession.

When William came down Steens was in the dining-room.

'Good morning.' Steens blew through his pleasant little

moustache, fanning it out. 'Yours is "on t'side".' He smiled one of his dimpling, multiple smiles. As always, he was clad in a suit, complete with waistcoat against the tweed of which gold glinted, mooring his chronometer. William could never remember if it had originally belonged to Captain Oates or to Amundsen. By dressing the way he did Steens managed to imply the pioneering of an Elton. At Fell Head he seemed one of the few rare migrants to receive any attention from Horton the Director, who lived twenty miles away, kept Civil Service hours and moved in an aura of Whitehall. One night Steens had elaborated on the fancy of Horton having been exiled to the wilds of Fell Head after some misdemeanour or following the fall of powerful relatives. He claimed to be working his way through all the classic Russian novels and in them apparently that sort of thing happened all the time.

William's bacon leapt across the table.

'Having trouble, Bill? I got mine direct from the hand of la Coulthard. Where's old Bellsize?'

'He went out collecting at dawn.'

'I admire Bellsize.'

'So you've said.'

'Well, don't you, William? You sounded a little surprised.'

'I hadn't thought about it.'

'You mean admiration should be rational? That's an interesting idea: quantified esteem.'

'I don't probably. It depends what you mean by admire.'

'I'd look it up but the library consists of some early *Country Life* and all forty volumes of the *Journal of Animal Ecology*. The story of our subject, William. Did you know Horton has something on today? Coulthard was bulling the tractor and Horton's been here for hours.' Steens smiled one of his knowing smiles—an expression of how-zat.

'I can never get over this place either. Those regulations about coffee-break and not brewing up over Bunsens. What did you say it was like?'

'A cross between Wuthering Heights and Porton Down.'

'You were right.'

'I don't know what your plans are but I think I shall take a long walk round the Reserve keeping an eye open for the old *Microtus*.'

'Have you found any yet?'

'To put no finer point on it, William, no. But I'm still looking. There's something rather pure about studying a species which doesn't appear to be present. Its absence might arguably be of significance to the ecosystem, but perhaps not enough. Which is why I'm off out of it. Even the politicians are beginning to have to make noises. I suspect some little man from the Department for the Environment may be heading this way. I shall tell him I'm working on a study of *Microtus absentis*. I shall then roundly accuse him of letting ICI poison the little perishers in order to swell Central Office funds. How about that?'

'I hope I'm there.'

Leaving the station William kept his eye open for visiting Brass. Now he saw the place through Steens's account of it. It was true that Horton ran things on strict Civil Service lines, though Mrs Coulthard ran them too—incivil lack of service in her case. Yet she was not an entirely negative factor like the *Microtus*. She was a local and part of the ecology of this high, soaked land, this secret land accumulating energy in the peat and living hand-to-mouth, secretive and miserly. Would such fancies appeal to Janet? Away from her his love for her welled clearer; he recognised the secrecy of his being, things concealed from himself. Fleetingly—a glimpsed and theoretical area. But, accounted for in terms of repression or more simply lack of active investigation, there it was.

Fancy ran out as it always did as the moorland grew under his walking eyes into an unprofuse richness—the drably undifferentiated of first sight laying out its specific balance of greys and jewellish greens and dark, hag-lipped pools plethorically converting energy in a hundred forms of life even here under a mostly numb sky. A hill or so away and giving right-

157

ful size to this deceptive landscape gleamed the bright speck of Bellsize after frogs. Bellsize alone amongst dull anoraks and para-military clobber wore a Helly-Hensen of shocking pink. Did he do it to give the frogs a sporting chance? Once William had seen him extending a great russet hand and clucking like a mother—the frogs were taken in. You had to give it to Bellsize.

Elsewhere Steens was to be seen by some sky-sized eye, Steens with his more cryptic coloration, his watch-chain and moustache. Steens was admirable too. He suggested long un-encumbered afternoons, *Three Men in a Boat*, safety. Whilst he shaved cicumspecting his moustache with such care and rubbed his gold links after supper with Kleenex, so long would famine and raging pestilence keep its distance. Bellsize and Steens moving across blanket bog—and himself, a third for the sky-sized eye. Three alone.

The moors imaged in six eyes.

Steens looking for absent mice, Bellsize magnetting frogs and Goodyear off to scoop up the tiny *Horobinia sphagnetorum* which in total possibly outweighed all the more spectacular species, an acre of them the biological equivalent of his finite self. What the world was to the other two, even this elemental manifestation, was not only unknown but unknowable. He felt better for that—if he'd felt worse at all in the first place. You had to be Bellsize to beat a bad breakfast and a bleak sky.

She'd have fed the children by now—Rupert the eater and Alice, creative player with Ready-Brek and egg.

The pioneer of his particular site must have liked walking. It lay far from the station on an unusual plateau. Sampling it seasonally allowed you a view of the moors in all their states. The winter had been the mildest on record and he'd had to eke out the tiny flurries of snow with the old timers' stories of Land-Rover disasters, frostbites and of Horton's arriving—even in sixty-two—on time, on skis.

As he walked William registered more than walking warmth and he saw the first rent of blue in the dark mirror of a pool. The weather shovelling over from the west was beginning to run out of moisture. His coat, loaded with ironware, became more of a burden, carried. Reaching the outcrop, he was glad to sit on a rock. A high solitude. The phrase drifted across his mind like a last tag of cloud, unconnected. It had him imagining for a moment what it might be like inside a poet's head—a facility for phrases, a *faculty* for them. High solitude was facile. He tried to recall poetry, anything, and got—

Winged something, loved of men,
Who could withstand your victory then.

But could place it only in one of Janet's Penguins. Now he held a general impression of his wife but hardly knew her. Measureless inadequacy of love, he thought. But the phrase this time was manufactured—and love was not quantifiable. 'How much do you love me?' was a question children asked. He was trying to remember if Rupert had asked it—it couldn't possibly be little Alice—when he discovered himself asking it and his mother saying 'A hundred pounds.' 'Not enough,' he said quietly to the moorland.

Now the sun was strong enough to redden his shut eyelids, or to implant a pinkishness. It was measurement again. Two miles away the solarimeter in the lab would be picking up. A dull sky clunked sullenly in the corner of the room, a bright one ticked; changeable weather like this shot to pieces the concentration of counters and measurers. The pulse kept its own accounts. William sat up and scanned the definite lines of the outcrop.

Not high, it was an island in the peat and rock enough to have a few short rakes. The rock was good; he fingered it and looked up. Twenty feet of it took his breath but not anyone could have done it. And he was rewarded with a large ledge, thick in vegetation and crowned with blowing Cloud Berry. *Rubus* was the genus but he was stuck for the specific. *Idaeus?* No, raspberry. His botany had always been shaky. Strawberry

159

blossoms resembled these—but strawberry was a different genus? Their whiteness wavered like grounded butterflies. Levering himself over the edge, he went towards them. Training nagged him. *Rubus* what? Identify this plant, this animal.

He fell into shrieking darkness, his shriek. It cuffed him once or twice but he didn't know that. He hit black water with a smash and water made the first sortable sound— *pluck, pluck*: water dripping under the ground. Panic had come and was over and he had hold in a crevice. Funnily, his mind seemed tossed high in the air. Light drizzled down a green hole, tinselling a shaft. It was almost perfectly round; it was a mining adit. Long ago they had mined for lead all over this area. According to Steens there were hundreds of miles of rock tunnels hacked by the hands of labour brought in to work hard and die young.

'God.' It had the timbre of a water-drop. *Pluck.*

Intricate little signals in his fingers relaxed as his feet landed on a firm rest and water reached only just above his knees. Some ten feet above hope of another ledge glimmered and higher still another. He had been right to keep his head then. He could wait here and then, when he was ready, climb stage by stage into the green air. Taking his time he listened to the resonant dropping of water. Interval and pitch were constant: an air on one string, expressing nothing.

Eight years since he had arrived too late for his father's death in a London room he saw now. That reclusive life had given him the slip. The landlady, London Scottish, still with time for people: 'He lived sparsely in every way.' And the picture of a girl, on the back of which: 'A *celui que j'aimerai toute ma vie.*' Unexplained. Echoless. Died.

'William Arthur Goodyear,' he named himself, trying immediately to avoid the funereal sound. Arthur was what Janet had called him, but not so much now.

He feared for her as if she was trapped and he was in the air. Also it was stupid to die here. Names checked by a reporter, age in brackets, 'Father of two young children.' Marriage was a rope for climbing, not binding. Increasingly he was convinced of the absurdity of dying this way. He was in control of himself! Adaptation to habitat; there was more fear blowing about the moor than down here in the shaft. Potentially agoraphobic, that was a datum for self-knowledge, a puzzle. And marriage like a rope or rockface, that was another new one. Marriage was something he had never thought about; it had never seemed an institution. But in the business of it perhaps they had grown to overlook each other?

All the people he knew or had known had never been so distinct, so separate in their lives; he glimpsed the great but fragile structure of all the connections between them. They all shone!

At the end of his reach he found a hold. The rock was irregular from hand-hewing but smoothly so and slippery with wet. All the few seconds he was sliding off and only a deep square hole saved him. Clamped to the new ledge, he could use nothing but his eyes which moved idly and at leisure over livid bits of timber. His body would refuse the next stage: it was numb with pains and it gasped round a vacuum. Getting upright, William nearly fell. He crawled to the good prospect of a jutting slab and arrived at the next stage twenty feet above water level almost with ease. Fifteen feet above him the green hole looking bigger; it looked near. The rock was clean-cut though and curving into overhang. Remembering something read, he guessed the shaft to have started as a bell-pit. A seam of the galena turned sideways by some spasm; a prospector a century or so ago taking his snap amongst Cloud Berry, picking up a lump.

This ledge was commodious, five feet in places and much lighter. William sat down to study his chances at leisure. Nil. Nil.

The walls were like cathedral work. Suddenly in a slant of light opposite he saw the date 1780 and the initials W. G. They were crisp and unweathered, they were his own initials. The date explained the pointless perfection of the work, before the London Lead Company and when Profit still wore a fair mask. The initials were coincidental and meaningless. He'd shuddered to see them. Odds against. But they could be hopeful, not fateful: evens on. Twenty-six times itself gave odds of 1:675, but less if you made adjustments for the rarity of Xenophon Yarboroughs. It was a cell with no floor in which he sat—he was a prisoner in a dungeon lit through a grille of stems, which was the oubliette he'd stepped through. An oubliette!

It was one of the things his father had told him. You stepped into what you had overlooked; you stepped and were forgotten.

Water dropped by, missing this ledge which was as dry as dust and was covered with dust. They were the water-drops echoing down where he dared look only because he had come from it. Lack of possibilities stunned him. It was unreasonable that there was no way, no route graded 'almost impossible'.

Shouts here might be heard by anyone near enough. But no one was. Bellsize would be bombing off to Brum, Steens ... perhaps. He came to see the only possibility, the non-alternative, was sitting it out. Keep warm. Catch the drops and drink them. Hour after hour after hour. Save shouting until long after tomorrow's dawn when Fell Head might be on the scent. There was Coulthard's intimate knowledge of the area, Horton's colonel-like powers of organisation and there was Steens, white teeth on pipe-stem, thinking it out behind his bland brow. And at the base of the outcrop lay the mute witness of his coat and gear. If only his coat was Bellsize-red! Taken all together, it was enough.

For half an hour or so—his watch had stopped—he sat sodden and bruised, feeding his brain initials. Start with A.A. Admiral Anson? Didn't count. He grasped after a great aunt: Arabella Adams. Adams was right, his mother's maiden name. M.A., M.G., M.S., she provided three for the price of one. G.A. was Janet's father and Hubert was H.A. Janet gave J.A. and J.G. but could you count married names? Six hundred and seventy-six: he had time to do them all and time to work out the rules. His mind began digging up people he hadn't thought of for years to get the initials. Gore in the old Cambridge lab. His first name was a blank. Impossible he'd never known it. There was also some unanswered query concerning Gore's future, now his past. It was marriage; had Gore ever married? It was simple to promise himself to find that out ... a solemn undertaking ... Gore would be in Zoology somewhere ...

He had to shake his head to make anything move inside it.

A very small spider to look at. Outside plants the incredibly numerous *Araneidae* had always been his biggest blank. Its eight legs searched for grip to negotiate a great projection scarcely big enough for a fingernail. Paper: The Natural History of a Prison Cell. The inevitable history of the oubliette. Try initials. Hope had gone out of that. All the A's. Spider sailed on his do-it-yourself parachute and tried again.

Let Gore be christened Walter to match the initials now in shadow.

Robert the Bruce. R the B. Why *the* Bruce, what was a bruce?

He cast around for the spider; it seemed to have given up.

He sneezed. His watch had stopped and he had caught cold. Cause and effect, it was as simple as that. Cause and effect terrified him.

He was learning about fear, its gaseous, liquid and solid states. Now after brushing and tickling it was on him, stuffing itself in like suffocation. There was starvation and slow madness and a racketing end in the pit. The secret dialogue with death was no longer whispered. Making no movement or sound he fought for his life. Each pore pushed out a cold drop. The hands at his face were his. He bit lightly at fingers and thumbs until some little comfort grew there and his mind settled in images of his children and Janet's body and he wondered if he was lost. Yet there were things to do, actions in reserve. Shouting for help for instance, working round the shaft to examine W.G. 1780.

First he removed his shirt and vest, wiping his torso with the vest. Scientific knowledge was confusing as to the benefit of that—he followed the general belief in getting wet clothes

163

off. Undressing carefully took time and he spread his gar-
ments fastidiously in the dust. He moved on all fours. At one
point the ledge had cracked away. The danger seemed pur-
poseful.

Once his tongue stuck to the dry roof of his mouth which
felt like the moon.

Crawling, he saw the small hole where the classic wains-
cot mouse-hole would be. It was precisely below the inscrip-
tion. It had the cut of a tomb but his bare chest proved a
draught. Air circulated then. He remembered to run his fingers
round the carving—W.G. 1780—then wriggled in head first.
The tunnel floor scoured his flesh and disappointed him by
being downwards. Soon there was no light—the passage was
too cramped for him to turn his head but the dark air was
still alive.

> Breathe on me breath of God,
> Make all my living pure.

W.G's tunnel went straight and even and widened to allow
him to turn, see distantly into the shaft and carry on his
retina a faint pincushion of light projecting ahead. Angle and
direction changed but he doubted his senses. He had great
trust in W.G. The mirage of light got stronger but light
could not be generated inside.

A sharp corner and light burst in his head. Slowly he went
up to it. He was at the foot of the outcrop with eyes only for
the light. He stepped into the miraculous furnace of the day.

'But what do your people actually do, Director?'

'Basic research,' said Horton. If he sighed it was lost in the
wideness of the Fell Head study area. Steens was enjoying his
morning; he had been seized for moral support and the look of
the thing. Horton added by way of translation—'The grass
roots stuff.'

'Not much of a grass up here.' The Visitor laughed, testing
the sphagnum with his shooting-stick. 'Wouldn't keep
horses.'

164

'That's probably correct, sir.' Horton's performance had been increasing in stature throughout the morning.

'An uncle of mine farmed near Newmarket once.' Steens watered his remark with a smile. The Visitor expressed interest but Steens deferred to the ever-shrewd Horton who had given him 'a look'.

'I've taken the liberty of arranging a little show of our bits of hardware. I.B.P. is using computers in the construction of the models and we've nothing like that here.'

'Glad to get away from them. More like malignant filing cabinets than anything else. Don't like them.'

'The temperature and humidity recorders of course we saw before coffee. They're the latest in met technology. In fact they were quite envious at Bracknell.'

'I hope you get some better results than they do. Henley last year, or was it 'sixty-nine? Absolute bloody fiasco.'

'Luckily the weather's the one thing we don't project.'

'Ought to,' said the Visitor. 'Be some sense in that. What do you mean "hardware", Horton? More Government expenditure, eh?'

'As you know, sir, we're very modest.'

'Not saying you're not.'

'Here comes the aerial collecting van now.'

A van bumped along the track, fixed to its roof a large collecting-net and what looked like a marine ventilator. It made an eight-point turn and rushed, bumping, back.

'Aerial sampling,' said Horton.

'Frighten the grouse.' The Visitor actually poked Steens in the ribs.

'It is at the experimental stage,' said Steens, again—fascinatingly—a slight false move: clearly Horton did not welcome such backing-up. In the far distance Coulthard could be seen running from the van.

'We've adapted an agricultural drill on this next item. The idea's to speed the soil sampling. This is straight out of the oven—I've been developing it personally.'

'Jerries had something similar in the War. Foxholes. All

165

right till it broke down when they'd find they had no shovels. Typical Jerry. What's the background thinking, Horton? You'll do you people out of a job with this. Research is labour-intensive, better not forget it.'

'It's merely an aid.'

'Thin end of the wedge. You'd do better sticking to people. The North's just getting over all those redundant pitmen. Don't want PhD's on every street-corner. Ha! Stick to people. That's from the shoulder and off the record.'

'I indented for wastepaper bins last Christmas and they haven't been passed to date.'

'I'll look into that. One item we can't get enough of, eh?' The Visitor again stabbed Steens, then, suddenly pleased, said: 'Nice set-up here, Director. Very businesslike.'

'We try to be,' Horton deftly tacked. 'Where's Coulthard and that tractor?'

'This your man?'

'Bill Goodyear.'

'One of ours?' Horton was alarmed.

'Rather an important species,' said Steens.

The Visitor chuckled with complex relish.

Goodyear was making straight for them. He was half dressed, black, scratched and white-haired with dust; he altogether resembled an elderly negro travelling the Underground Railroad.

THREE

'Last day to ourselves.' Janet placed the drinks, ice jangling, on the garden bench. He took her hands, surprising himself— almost as if Death and not twenty-one degrees centigrade was in the air. 'Oops, are you going to propose?'

'Not specially. Kids all right?'

'They're out here with you, aren't they?'

He stood on the bench. 'They're in that sunken garden. The owner seems to specialise in building ancient monuments.'

'What sort of stone is it? It's almost red like that whatsit city, half as old as time. Rose-red city.'

'Sandstone.'

'I always thought it was the other way—sand being made by eroded stone.'

'This is stone made by cementation of sand. It's had a long time.'

'I suppose it has. It's the same stuff as the rocks. When I went there with Rupert we found dozens of names and dates. Boys from the school, going right back. It was funny. They're all jumbled. Erosion.'

'Did you see the Isle of Man?'

'No, but you can—I asked in the village. They said when you couldn't see it it was raining and when you could it was a bad sign.'

'But you couldn't and it's not raining.'

'So much for folk-wisdom.'

'Unless you weren't looking in the right direction.'

'You look then.'

'Sorry.'

'Don't apologise.'

'Sorry.'

Unexpectedly, she grabbed him round the waist. 'Are you being infuriating, thick or just married?'

He kissed her. 'You ought to know by now. I'm being apologetic.'

'I don't want an apology for a husband.'

'Did I tell you about the date carved in the mine.'

'Several times but go ahead. It was fascinating, you being superstitious. The big rational Bertrand Russell thing has blown away and we're all the same as ever.'

'Can I have that in writing?'

'Just because I try to initiate a bit of intelligent conversation. How many are coming? We'll be washing up the whole time. I'd rather with all the good stuff they've got. She must collect antiques. My brothers break things and your sister I can't see doing vast amounts, though she might. It's a proper family reunion and if I remember my T. S. Eliot it'll end up with furies howling at the french windows.'

William watched them from the high window, Alice in her push-chair, holding Prof, which was nearly as big as herself and a cross between a teddy and something else, and Rupert trailing his metal spade. The hideous Beachcote Hotel was having its morning shadow thrown on carparks lying like fishponds between it and the sea. Today the island was visible, its peaks floating on the forty-mile horizon. Rupert's spade trickled faintly up to him. These three were his and only a week or so ago he had seen them lost for ever. Alice clutched Prof, Rupert stomped dutifully to work at sandcastles and his forty-second cousin, his wife—face blobbish at the distance—looked up and waved. He waved back. Eight years married already was hard to believe.

Closing the window, he tried to gauge the tide but the sea's edge was obscured by carpark walls and notices. Even to his improving but still slightly defective vision the Isle of Man was sharp as a cut-out of black paper. Folk wisdom held that as a bad sign. The folk were pessimistic, justly perhaps—not

168

counting their chickens, suffering many a slip; but clouds came silver-lined on winds that were never ill. The folk were non-committal.

He straightened the bed. This room was three times as big as theirs at home, with furniture to match—glossy as conkers.

He stretched as wide as the bed, thinking of the shore before breakfast which the sea had left ready for the day, after that sharp night storm, in a perfect gradation of variously sized washed pebbles. It was a demonstration of a precision in its brute force he had not recognised before.

Having been left to work, he felt conscience urging him to begin. Work. It was proofs for *The Entomologist*, sufficiently exacting to give him an impression of accomplishment but mechanical enough to leave him on holiday. A gale blew through the house, panicking doors. Mrs Barbour in her instructions had a paragraph about the inner and outer front doors which advocated an airlock method of entry. It was the postman. 'It's a laal holiday from their dog,' he said. 'If you're Goodyear this is yours. This for them's a final notice but they paid afore they went, so you won't be cut off.'

His letter in a writing he did not know was marked 'Personal'; the Barbours' he put behind the clock. He spread the proofs on the kitchen table, taking a moment to breathe the urgent savour of printed galleys which faded in the journal and became untraceable in piled offprints. When the letter rustled in his back pocket he removed and opened it. The address was peculiarly familiar—next door's at home; the name on page three was Sheila Mumford. He read:

Dear William,

We are off but I expect Janet has told you about it. Wasn't it sudden? Robert got that promotion at last and we are moving to Godalming, the South again. It's in Surrey, the selecter part, with prices to match! I have been thinking for ages whether to write this and it's only because you are such a reasonable man and I could always talk to you that I am writing. I am also writing because I was very fond

169

of Janet as well. I do not know what I would have done without the friendship of both of you. It made Manchester livable and I hope we will be as lucky next time. So often these days marriages go on the rocks, what starts as a crack you can paper over ends as divorce and I don't want to think of it happening to you. With you being away on your 'research' I haven't had time to speak to you. It was what made my mind up to write when I realised I would have *said* this to you. You may be wondering now what it is. Well, do you remember just after you went away Janet was going to a party. I definitely knew you knew this— wasn't it some university people? I have always been good at observation and she was definitely under some sort of strain. This is what I wanted you to know. I can't say why but I can say what, nerves. After the party Janet came home with a man who stayed till morning. I expect you know about this but when I invited her to talk openly ('thera-peutic', I think is the word and confess I looked it up!) she was *not* herself and 'snapped my head off'. I was worried because she *is* such a special person. You don't need me to tell you that! All this anarchy and loss of direction can bring on confusion and its special people like Janet who always get the brunt of it. I am now sure in my own mind that it is right to put you in the picture.

Very sincerely yours,

Sheila (Mumford).

He tore it across and across into the size of postage stamps. A door slammed somewhere and the pieces rose as at a gun-shot, falling everywhere. Carefully he gathered them up and stuffed them in the scuttle under coal thoughtfully provided by the owners. Then he wiped his fingers.

The proofs were going to be more exacting, less mechanical.

'Haven't you got them to bed yet?'

'No, I haven't. Rupert's lost his pyjamas.'

'No one's lost anything. They're in the airing-cupboard. You know where that is, don't you?'

'I've looked.'

'Do you want me to do it?'

'No, I'll do it.'

Stairs again to find that Alice had wet herself. Pyjamas, fallen beside tank, offered.

'Not *those*. They're *stupid*.'

'Put them on. Stop being childish. Put them on, Rupert.'

'All right.' Centuries of resignation.

In the garden the effects of the sea-wind to work out and the owner's wiles to get more delicate plants to grow. One wizened rose, blighted by salt—itself the breeding-ground of two or three ailments—he christened 'the Sheila Mumford'. Slowly suspicion was moving in and pushing out his first reactions. That was the way with poisons and blights. With no collusion from him, the coal-scuttle had become the centre of the house. He had almost questioned Rupert—you know the man who had breakfast, did you like him? Modelled out on his son's forehead expressive puzzlement—'what are you talking about?' or—latest school phrase—'you're going nutty'. He hadn't. He'd had too much of that sort of thing himself. Sheila was a vindictive bitch, not surprising in retrospect. Better to ask Janet outright. That man you had for breakfast, did you like him? Soon he'd be piecing the letter together. At a certain stage, the poison demanded feeding. I had a letter today ... Simple. What would happen on her face then?

'There's Hubert. Who on earth's that with him? She looks foreign.'

'The sea, it is marvellous. We are like seabirds.'

'Isle of Man.' After three days William felt proprietorial. 'That's Scotland on the north horizon.'

'L'Ecosse. That's fantastic.'

'Monique comes from Bordeaux. The oceanic type.'

'What's that? Oh, I see, you are being funny.' Monique stuck out her tongue.

'We must be about two-hundred feet above sea-level here.' Detailed to take them for a walk, William felt obliged to furnish information.

'Hubert has never been to France, so how can he be civilised?'

'I don't claim to.'

'Do you know the area, *les Landes*?'

'Sand and scrub, isn't it?'

'Exactly. Not like this. You get no elevation. The sea is unvariable. Here it is aglint. You see the vastness.'

'About two thousand square miles.'

'Bill's a scientist.'

'Everything measured?'

'Everything that's measurable,' he said, to defend himself. She took the distinction : she was quick, attentive. He began to feel glad for Hubert. She was an *assistante* at his school somewhere near Birmingham; they were colleagues, probably lovers as well. He felt the draw of France and of her being younger, coming back with a start to his suppressed ache, forgetting it again.

Hubert said : 'It's like a great lake.'

The sea pricked with shifting lights was confined by mountains on the rim, huge but not threatening infinity. Guillemots moved from element to element; man's various going concerns along the coast huddled under their little fogs.

Janet asked him in a whisper if fennel was good for stews. She had put in various things, trying to lift the dish a star or two. He knew it was because Monique was French and affection inflicted a pang. She gave no evidence at all to corroborate the Mumford letter. But his mother had given no evidence.

Monique disappeared upstairs with Rupert two minutes after he had wandered down.

'Hang on to that girl,' said Janet. 'I don't think she is but you know how most girls are brought up in France—out to catch you I mean. Of course it is easier to be good with children before you have any.'

'I'll remember all that. She is good with kids. The Sixth Form like her.'

'I bet. The boys will. I could never understand what French-women see in Frenchmen. Perhaps French men take care they never see any other brand.'

'Which is why they're so touchy about letting us join the boring old E.E.C.'

'Because we have hair on our chest.'

'Speak for yourself.'

'I was speaking for you, dear. I don't suppose you remember when you were a little boy of thirteen and I had to look sideways to see yours.'

'I've repressed that. You'd flash round pictures of me on a fur rug.'

'I would if I had one. She'd be tickled pink. Little boys are sweet in small doses.'

'I'm a sour old English master now, complete with a subscription to the *Critical Quarterly*. Are we ready to eat?'

'You are, but we're not all here.'

'Bill's only gone to the Beachcote to get some wine.'

'Bill's loving sister hasn't though.'

'Is *she* coming?'

'You don't sound delighted.'

'I'd rather not meet her on an empty stomach, that's all.'

'I've always thought you got on with everyone.'

'You've always had a soft spot for me.'

'Bill as well then.'

'I like Bill.'

'You always saw the good in everyone. Your great gift to see good. When I saw good in people it was often through you. I couldn't bear it if you stopped.'

'You could; there's very few things people can't bear. For heaven's sake don't cry, Janny love. You've put the salt in.'

* * *

173

'Do you think they're all right?'

'They've got enough bedding for a hospital.'

'That was a good idea of yours to send them up to the attics. They can do what they like up there.' She yawned. 'Though they must be too tired to do anything. I'd never have thought we'd have had any qualms about asking them. Still, you can't say—do you sleep together? I can't. That's what marriage must be for.'

'What's marriage for?' William spoke from his shirt.

'So that you know what to do with your guests.'

'Oh, I see.'

'You get solemn on holidays. I've noticed it before.'

By the time he was out of his shirt she was a hump in the bed. She could do things quicker than he could and sometimes fell asleep in mid sentence. He yawned and scratched himself in the flank of the wardrobe. No veneer could produce that depth in wood. Downstairs in the coal-bucket lay the shredded evidence. No impulse of his ever worked out. Easy to have passed over the letter without comment but impossible to hold out a handful of sooty scraps. It was a fatal illness he was keeping from her but the effects were opposite: negating. In bed he reached across her breathing softness. She gave his hand a perfunctory squeeze. Marriage was full of habits, scarce in protestation. That was all right. Wave after wave came sawing at the shore. He lay unsleeping.

Janet abruptly changed buttock to take in the other side of the lake. He yelped for her to steady on. Dark waters were champing inches from the plywood gunwale. Big to get on a roof-rack, the dinghy floated like a cockleshell. 'It's the deepest. It's as deep as the Screes are high.'

'Are those the Screes? It's almost like a ruled line where they meet the water.'

'And go on the same underneath for more than a thousand feet.'

'Incredible. I'll sit still and you can take me to Avalon. Watch out for arms clad in white, shrinkproof samite.'

174

'It's looking like rain.'

'Arthurian heroes don't notice such things.'

'I bet they did,' he said. 'You can see the bottom this side.'

'I daren't move.'

'You can your head.'

'Waterweed.'

'I like your knees.'

'After all these years? They're just knees.'

'No, they're more than that.'

'I'd kiss you but it would be immediate double suicide. Do you realise Rupert went up there this morning? Now she's got both of them—she deserves the *Légion d'Honneur* at least. I don't know if he found them together or not, but it accounts for our lie-in.'

It was a reminder, the cue he could not take. William rowed on over the rocky bed. When everything was a reminder and speech impossible he would have gone down for the last time—obsession complete, spiritual paralysis absolute. Yet, even now, he wondered if he wasn't having to work at it a bit—if, given leave, his spirit would not disperse into surroundings, hanging about in the gullies on Gable, dipping with the oars into the dark bulk of Wastwater.

The rain which had been holding off half morning let go, Lake District rain—always less a change in the weather than a modulation. Its drops hitting the water plucked and circled it making everywhere the exact likeness of nipples erect. On her face it ran through her hair and fanned over her forehead gathering again into a running meldrop down her nose. As sometimes he glimpsed possibilities—whole other landscapes as a geologist might from some chipped-off clue in his hands—now he glimpsed some large sensual potentiality from the way his wife's face was letting the rain net it. And he gripped the small and rebellious oars, hurting his hands on them.

Some sort of hailing shout through the rain. Two stood on the little promontory they had set out from, neither Hubert nor Monique. Both were tall and one held a golfing umbrella.

'Only your sister would dress like that.'

He looked over his shoulder as he brought the dinghy in, not seeing how she was dressed but perfectly believing Janet was right. Any ideas of suitable attires he may once have had lay floundered in the nineteen-sixties. 'Who's with her?'

'Hard to tell.' But he believed she knew.

'You do the strangest things in the provinces.' Tricia was wearing a crinoline and a cloche hat. She spoke almost affectionately.

'Long time no see.' The other was Jack looking no fatter, greyer, balder—Jack dressed in a suit hand-tailored from hem to hem and enshrining indubitably, overwhelmingly, every virtue advertising bore witness to. Casually, he was the advertised man. 'How are you doing?'

Finding that unanswerable they scrambled out of the Barbours' boat, soaking themselves.

'We got delayed,' said Tricia. 'Otherwise we'd have shacked up with you last night, wouldn't we, darling? We country-housed in Lancs. Jack knows some terrible people these days, don't you, dove? But we didn't want to let the opportunity go by on the M6 so here we are. That note on the door *was* thoughtful.'

'How are you, Janet? You look nice.'

'That's me. You look fit.'

'Made my day. Squash.'

'Are we invited to lunch?' Tricia stroked William's cheek, which he found a cold and unexpected touch. 'Driving since dawn. We've got some wine in the boot, one that really travels.'

'My very words.' Jack took over. 'No, she's got children and everything. Couldn't we all go for a drink somewhere, and a meal? Where's Cockermouth?'

'We were expecting you.'

'But that was just me,' said Tricia slyly.

'Janet's right.' William patted Jack's arm. 'There's enough to feed an army.'

*   *   *

'I expect you were a teeny bit surprised. Jack's re-materialisation after all this time?' Tricia was, after all, helping with the dishes.

'I'd never thought he'd de-materialised.'

'I see. His re-emergence then.'

'Not particularly then.'

'You must have! It's only natural. Just imagine old Caradoc re-materialising. One does have some interest in the people one's been to bed with. Don't be so disappointing.'

'I'm sorry. I think we've nothing in common now, if we ever had.'

'If you want to know, I think he never quite got over you.'

'What's that supposed to mean?'

'It's just simple English. He was studying you all through lunch, wasn't he?'

'That's just nonsense.'

'Eyes for nothing else.'

'I must have been too busy with Alice.'

'Don't use that argument! You're really not a bit convincing. Some people might be cut out to be parents and nothing else. You're not. William's all right—he's my brother! But between ourselves there are more engrossing men.'

'I don't admit anything you say.'

'That's bigoted.'

'I'm not interested.'

'In what?'

'Your spite I suppose.'

'Not very friendly. It's not only what I say you refuse to admit. You won't admit what's becoming common knowledge almost. We're all on the look-out for what impression we make. Exhibitionism if you like. You cling to the good old virtues, don't you? Like fidelity for instance when they're based on bad old self-deceptions. No, let me finish. I wonder you didn't point out that I married a man called Foster a few years ago. You had the invite but you didn't come. Was that what shocked you?'

'I'm suitably impressed.'

'You haven't changed, have you? You're still exactly the same clever Cousin Janet.'

'Leave them to drain.'

'Take a pew, Janet. You did the washing up bit.'

'Thank you, Jack. We shared it.'

'Take a settee then.'

'Yes. I will seat myself on the floor. Hubert can tell you it is what I usually do.'

'At his feet? Lucky man.'

'English gallantry at its best,' said Tricia.

'Because of French wine at its best then.'

'*Enchantée*. It was nice. All we can afford is the Spanish "plonk".'

'When we're in the Common Market ...'

'Well?'

'I don't know,' said Hubert. 'But they've started discussing it in the staff room and that always gets me worried.'

'Do you remember Cuba?'

'Do I remember Cuba? I was an undergraduate. Sorry, sis, carry on.'

'I was just going to say that when Cuba was on I heard quite ordinary people talking about it on a bus. I mean they usually don't. That's when I lost my nerve.'

'I can't remember the date,' said Jack. 'But it was when I always asked myself what you'd think or say about anything. I did, you know, for one, two years?'

Tricia snapped her fingers. '*In vino veritas* ought to be Jack's motto.'

'It's true.' Monique was being quick to rectify a wrong diapason. 'In France there is quite a bit more talk like that on buses.'

'They talk French in France.'

'*Oui, oui.*'

Rupert sniggered. 'What's that?'

'It is French. You must go to an advanced school, Rupert,

where they teach you it in the infants.'

'Worth it at that.' Jack was man-to-man. 'In the design trades we're on a winner. More trips all round to Paris. Glasgow unfortunately is where the mills are.'

'Do you own mills now?'

'Not quite. Almost, Janny, almost. From rags to riches and you went and left after Act One. That's not fair. It never was from rags. Fits your tale more, Trish.'

'What's that about my tail? One thing he can't do is drink.'

'Don't listen to her. She—oh and you, Bill, of course had this genuine slum grandmother. Right? She's been dusting that side of the ancestry. You should hear her brown teapots. And the picture of "t'owd man" in his shirtsleeves over the hearth. Am I right?'

'The typical wrong detail. Any picture of grandpa would have certainly been in number one dress. She had her pride, didn't she, William? Good prole stock.'

'We didn't know her.'

'Yes, we did. We went there when we were small. I remember, so you must—you're older.'

'She wasn't anything you say.'

'I'm not ashamed of it. Common ancestors are acceptable anyway and you more or less can't be anything but socialist now. Under a certain age. Even all the debby types, for what that's worth.'

'It started at this smart party at Blackheath where there was a socialist ex-Minister or an ex-socialist Minister. Anyhow that's when your granny walked again.'

'Don't listen to him.'

'Wisdom of Simple Folk, Trish. Oh yes, that's what got him on to Opinion Polls.'

'Someone's got to have some or it's a poor outlook. Experts don't.'

'Yes, I agree with Hubert,' said Janet. 'We have the usual quota of planners' dreams at home—and as usual, nightmares for everyone else.'

179

'People are the most plastic substance known,' said Jack. 'Mark my words, manipulation is in its infancy.'

There was some general protest and he waved a friendly hand. 'I don't say I necessarily hold with it. It's a fact of life.'

'A short-term one,' said Hubert. 'There's no *body* in this sort of conception of life. You look at any general assumptions from the past—say the turn of the century—and most of the generally held assumptions don't bear looking at. What most people believe is wrong, is that it? and what they feel is likely to be right?'

'It's entirely governed by the section that makes the running, is and probably always was,' said Jack. 'Now it's more self-conscious, more scientific in fact. What I said—Manipulation is the blushing new science.'

'Who are the nine muses now, I wonder?' Monique spoke from the floor where she was helping Rupert with his jig-saw.

'Coffee?'

There was a general laugh. 'That's one.'

'May as well,' said Jack. 'You were always good at coffee. The Merc. is pretty easy but you never know about breath-alysers on a Sunday. What we haven't done is ask Bill for the scientist's view. Wasn't Science on the original panel?'

Tricia said: 'If I know him he'll qualify anything he might say out of existence.'

'Scientific view of what?'

'I told you!'

'Give the man a chance. This after-dinner debate: Manipulation versus the opinion of the man in the Clapham snarl-up.'

'I don't know.'

'There you are again!'

'No, you aren't,' said Janet. 'None of us damn well knows.'

'It's difficult.' Hubert seemed to be tying knots in Monique's hair. 'It's probably a non-question or something. But to have *un*manipulated stuff coming in is important. What encourages me is how life still manages to be messy and incomprehensible. *Itself*, it's somehow never clear or logical.'

180

'Owch!' He had apparently pulled Monique's hair. 'He is torturing me because I am French.'

'There might be a comparison from ecology,' said William, 'if that's what you want. Man lives on the credit of things no one thinks about, of plankton for example. Even the man on the Clapham omnibus must know that now. And I suppose there might be an unseen fund of decency in people and perhaps that's being squandered too.'

He returned in his mind to Hubert and Monique and whether they would marry. It was Janet's opinion and the last words exchanged. She was two hundred yards away. The simplicities of the vast uncovered beach and a still, lapping sea were devilled with a most spectacular sunset. There was beauty she would say was corny if he drew her attention to it. He valued her opinion and was glad for Hubert. His own sister had bustled off. People lived their lives.

Consciously now he lifted his eyes from the exposed pools where clusters of mussels formed grotty reefs and might get a geiger-counter excited and where dead crabs were too numerous—or had they died naturally? The sky was everything at once and man's corniness too slight to alter it. It was blue and green and red and three layers of cloud-formation went their own ways. Everything became tangible to him—he measured and contained it. Tearing the letter had been his first, and truest gesture. Half an hour ago he had determined to ask her outright—and had found the strength for it. Now not doing so had somehow been determined for him; he had found another strength in his nature to move away from it at another level.

Walking towards the sea they slowly converged.